Sydney and Calvin Have a Baby

by Adrienne Thorne

STARMAKER BOOKS

GRACEWATCH MEDIA

1

THIS IS A STORY of a guy, and a girl, and a baby. Of the three of us, it's rather possible that even the baby is better equipped to tell the story than I, considering that the infant in question possesses his mother's innate ability with the written word. Which, if we're being honest, is a pretty outstanding ability. I, on the other hand, while always having loved a decent read well enough, have never considered myself in any way skilled at writing. But as one party in this equation of ours is still, in fact, a gurgling bundle of soiled nappies, the duty of recounting this tale has fallen to me. Because, despite Sydney's skill in matters such as these, she has resolved ever more to stick solely and entirely to fictional accounts, for reasons you shall come to understand very soon.

Though her story began quite some time earlier, the train wreck of events that really got the ball rolling started in the hallway of her high school, St. Aloysius Academy. This particular Catholic school was one of those uniform-clad institutions that might make a pass at religious instruction here or there, but you'd probably never guess it if you walked the halls. Just now, Sydney Camden's experience was about to become a case in point.

Today was the day an especially significant banner was to go up. Currently, the drama students were hanging it with painstaking care, asking their spotter whether it needed to go just a bit higher on the left, and having no idea of the tumult they were causing in the life of one poor, brilliant nerd of a seventeen-year-old girl.

The banner read, SPRING PRODUCTION: *IN THE END* —A PLAY BY SYDNEY CAMDEN. Spelled out distinctly for the entire student body to see. This banner-hanging should probably have been a triumphant moment for Sydney. But it was decidedly not.

When she had determined to go all out and write a full-length play as her English term project last semester, she had expected a typically outstanding grade, perhaps some constructive but gentle criticism if she was lucky (or the assurance that not a thing about it needed changing if she was *really* lucky—but no need for crazy dreams here). What she definitely hadn't expected, though, was for her enthusiastic English teacher to send her play straight to the drama teacher, and for these two teachers to then agree that it should be performed as the spring production. The matter had been all but decided before she'd even given them the go-ahead. And certainly they'd had no reason to suspect she would hesitate. Because an actual, real performance was every playwright's dream, was it not?

Apparently, it was not. Because, though she'd gone along with it and given consent for her play to be performed,

Sydney rightly suspected that it was going to make her social life that much more hellish. Not that she had a habit of wallowing in its hellishness, exactly. But even though she rather tended toward a general absorption in the stories she was writing and creating throughout her daily life, the hellishness of her social life was pretty hard to miss.

Let's take a peek at her backstory and see just why this was the way of things for her, shall we?

Ever since she was a small child, Sydney had had one passion in life: writing stories. She had not chosen it so much as it had chosen her. As a very little girl, she had composed stories in her head long before she could physically write them, and she had (probably quite precociously) requested her mother supply her with a voice recorder so that she would be able to compose these masterpieces of hers in appropriate privacy without the necessity of a cumbersome, kid-to-mom dictation. At age four.

Once she learned how to use a pen and paper, the tales flowed all the more. She began with simple stories of princesses and gallant heroes saving them, of fighting dragons and adventure, perhaps a few modeled after her favorite Disney movies. But it wasn't long before the quality of her writing was well beyond that typical of her age.

Her parents didn't quite know what to make of all this (we'll get to them shortly), but her aunt, her very favorite Aunt Lisa who was about to graduate college with a writing degree at the time, hopped right onto the task of getting this little prodigy published. It turned out to be a very simple task to accomplish and served to whet Sydney's appetite for success in her apparently destined field.

Being caught up in her world of stories did, of course, make it a bit difficult for Sydney to find friends at school. And her loneliness only fed her desire to write beautiful, moving stories of friendship and love, in a completely unconscious desire to fill the void.

Really, by mid–grade school, despite having a few friendly acquaintances here and there, she'd only ever had one friend: a girl named Kendall. But alas, this friendship was destined to come to a smashing halt after a very brief time.

Kendall and Sydney got along quite well around age eight for the span of twenty-six days at the start of the school year, until Sydney unintentionally but quite thoroughly pissed Kendall off by earning their teacher's massive praise for a short play they'd each been assigned to write. It was a wonderful moment for Sydney, as she realized how much she loved the dramatic form. But Kendall was not used to being out-shown in any area of life, and certainly not accustomed to sharing the praise of her teachers. So when Sydney's play blew Kendall's clearly out of the water, as evidenced by their teacher's truthful and enthusiastic response, Kendall had to console herself somehow. This is how she did it: "Well at least I don't have to wear glasses and have terrible frizzy hair, and at least I can have as many friends as I want since I'm not obsessed with writing stupid stories. That's like all she's good for." And in a strange way, Kendall's mean words, spoken not directly *to* Sydney but to another student quite clearly loud enough for Sydney to overhear, became a sort of prophesy, in that hearing them caused Sydney to lose what little confidence she had in her ability to make friends.

Sydney's pursuit of writing began to take on a new level of almost frantic study. For she was not the type to stand up to someone like Kendall, nor necessarily to even acknowledge that Kendall had caused her pain. But young Sydney would certainly be darned before she'd ever let anything get in the way now of what was clearly, to her, her one purpose in life.

By the time she got to middle school her social life was looking bleak, and her advanced brain power was making standard public-school classes tearfully boring. So, briefly, her mother tried a stint of homeschooling. Despite this improving the tearful boredom issue as she was now able to jump into such things as a college-level study of Shakespeare, it caused other problems. Like a massive clashing of personalities between Sydney and her mother. Her mother, never having anticipated raising such a single-minded and intense daughter, tried to micromanage Sydney into broader pursuits, including areas of social interaction that Sydney had long ago concluded were beyond her. And Sydney, for her part, had a terribly difficult time treating her mother like a teacher and instead just felt irritated at her mother's increased controllingness. So after then suffering through one more year of public junior high, Sydney was relieved to finally enter high school at St. Aloysius, a private college-preparatory academy that she assumed would be an oasis of academic challenges.

Even though by the age of fourteen she was developing a few normal-person side interests—late '90s pop music already nearly out of vogue by the year she was born, for one; and experimenting with making her hair less frizzy, for another—she was still extremely devoted to her craft of writing. The school was obviously Catholic, but at that point in her life she cared very little one way or another about such things as religion. Her main excitement at entering St. Aloysius was that she hoped to find a student body similarly interested in academia. It was just possible that she wouldn't be the lone smarty-pants anymore and might even grow in her skill from the challenge that being surrounded by intellectual equals could offer.

How wrong she was.

Not only did her childhood frenemy Kendall come along and join her there, but Sydney also met a whole slew of similarly ill-behaved teenage Catholics. The school's academics were certainly an improvement and a welcome challenge, but socially speaking, things were as bad as ever. At least initially.

Two weeks into her first semester, however, things took a promising turn in the form of one Winnie Smith. The two of them had no initial spark of friendship until their English teacher purposefully paired them for a research project on Victorian poetry. Purposefully, because Winnie was already on track to fail the class, while Sydney was running academic circles around everyone.

Winnie was a bit of a strange creature. Even in everyday life matters, Winnie was anything but a genius, though perhaps made to seem even less so in comparison to her new friend. The Watson to Sydney's Sherlock, if you will. But the strange thing was that, though Sydney was clearly Winnie's intellectual superior, Winnie had at least quite a few of the makings of a popular girl and yet chose to hang with Sydney. Whether it was gratitude for that early passing English grade or that simple but inexplicable synergy of personalities that can happen sometimes, the two of them had been bestest chums ever since that first project together.

And now, on this worst of all mornings that should have been glorious for Sydney, she was ever so grateful to have a friend like Winnie.

The two of them were presently staring at the all-im-portant banner. But they quickly started walking away, no words needed between the two of them to discuss that their goal should be avoiding any extra attention drawn to the banner.

But that mattered little. Everyone saw it. As if to prove

this, a slew of immaturely malicious jocks were joking just loud enough for her to overhear:

"That's her, isn't it? Author of *In the End*?"

"Wonder what it's about. You think like the end of her shot at a sex life?" Followed by hilarious laughter.

Sydney's face clouded, her heart plummeted, and she fought the urge to look back at them. Fought it valiantly. Pretending the joke didn't sicken her, she said quietly to Winnie, "It's not even clever. Just immature."

Winnie, having no real convictions on whether Sydney was correct or not, was all support: "Totally. They should *grow up* already," aimed loudly in the offending jocks' direction.

The unfortunate thing was that all this distracted Sydney enough that she didn't see Kendall's slyly placed foot.

Sydney went down, blushing terribly as she tried to right herself. And Kendall went straight to a look of fake pity. "Oh, poor Sydney. Must be too distracted thinking up her little stories to watch where she's going." Before Sydney could get about ignoring this, Kendall went on, ostentatiously announcing, "Guys, watch out! Give her room! Don't get in her way or you'll block her muse!"

Winnie immediately grabbed Sydney's arm in support, snapping to Kendall, "Jealous much?"

To which Kendall responded by increasing the nasty: "Oh that's right. I'm so jealous of all *that*." And she subtly advanced with each word: "I'm jealous of her frizzy hair, and her zits, and her glasses. And her giant, giant brain."

Sydney tried her darnedest to keep from reacting. In her mind and her will, Sydney was stone, as strong as any heroine she'd ever written of, from her recent work all the way back to her Disney-imitation days.

But her outward demeanor couldn't quite reach such lofty heights. As Kendall smugly backed off, Sydney couldn't help but zip away into a nearby bathroom as the only way to ensure that no one would see if she started crying despite her near-heroic efforts at sealed tear ducts. Behind her, she could hear Winnie cussing Kendall out, but it did little to hearten Sydney. She knew there was only one thing to be done to ensure she returned to her outwardly placid, unconcerned self in the matter of minutes she had until the next period.

The bathroom was mercifully empty. Sydney went inside a stall anyway. And she got out her notebook.

She put pen to paper and got started.

It wasn't so much that she was rewriting her present circumstances just then. She'd tried that in the past, somewhere around age twelve when she'd placed a character who was literally herself into a lovely and happily ended story, one in which the heroine found a perfect true love slash guy best friend and had plenty of the sort of laughs and fun and quality time that made her heart happy. And, lovely as that story had been, writing it had seriously started to mess with Sydney's head. She had quickly discovered that she could only put so much of herself into her characters before her reality started to get a little hazily intertwined with theirs. It had tripped her out, and she had learned her lesson. For the time being.

So now, instead of writing something like that, all she was doing was jotting down some details of the new plot she had been concocting. Something very Jane Austen–esque with a terribly happy ending. Even if she couldn't insert herself per se into the story, she could still immerse herself in something happy in the hope that her own life would someday take such a turn, and that hope might be more than sufficient distraction from her present strife.

It worked. As she'd known it would.

When Winnie popped in to the loo a few moments later, Sydney was more or less herself again. "Syd? Are you okay?"

"Never better," she exaggerated, shoving her notebook back into her bag and emerging from the stall.

"Big talker," Winnie said, falling in with her as they headed back to the hall.

"What bitchy tormentor? What embarrassing banner? Nothing to see here," Sydney bantered back, her spirits lifting.

"Maybe you should just like make a list. Of who I need to tell off or get back at? And I'll come up with their punishments."

"That doesn't sound creepy or Unabomber-ish at all."

They were nearly parting ways at a fork in the hall. "Text it to me in class!" Winnie said by way of goodbye.

"Very funny," Sydney called to her, because they both knew that Sydney's nerdily serious devotion to academia would never allow her to be distracted by her phone in class, while Winnie regularly made an art of it.

Winnie waved and trotted away to her classroom. Sydney continued on through the near-empty hallway toward her own, and her mood was so much improved by the combination of her story and Winnie's light, fun friendship that it rather changed her outlook on life for the moment. So much so that the bizarre and amazing event that was coming her way would feel suspiciously legitimate.

2

SOME RATHER DREARY BUSINESS on Sydney's end was about to get underway, though she didn't know it yet. So let's skip to something happier for a moment… Or perhaps my mother's deathbed.

I was sitting in a London hospital beside her, both of us still in a bit of shock that this was happening to us so quickly. We'd had a good seventeen and three quarters years together, all alone in a way, she and I. We'd had about as happy a life together as a teenage chap and his single mum could have, and we had always gotten on together quite a bit better than the average pair in our state of life might have. And now it was to come prematurely to a close. A mere seven weeks ago she'd been diagnosed with advanced uterine cancer. The doctors had given her a month, and she'd been hanging on, neither one of us quite ready to let go.

Just now, she was going on through the pain and drugs, trying to plan out the rest of my life for me. We'd had a bit of time, very small bit, to discuss it before she got to this rather agonized point, but she was intent on making sure I was clear on the details once again now.

It seemed she had a sister. Who knew. Certainly not me, as the closest thing to extended family I'd ever encountered at this point was the old woman next door to our flat who'd been fond of giving me lollies and pinching my cheeks since the days when my cheeks had had pinchable chub. Certainly no one with our blood.

But impending death can unlock worlds of secrets, and in those odd number of days we had, between when we knew and the big *d*-day, my mother's lips became magically unsealed.

There were two of them, her sister Jem and herself. Twins, if you can believe it. I almost couldn't. You shared a womb, but have had no contact for the duration of my entire lifetime? What is wrong with you, woman? Apparently a lot.

Mum had gotten pregnant with me at seventeen. By some man she could barely speak of without a grimace. When I'd asked about him at times in the past, she had typically changed the subject and otherwise indicated that she was about as likely to take up the trapeze professionally as she was to tell me all about him. But on one rare occasion, she had indulged me with the information that he was an irresponsible sort of fellow, none too keen on the idea of my being born at all. The bugger. And that was essentially all I had ever known about him or the circumstances of my birth.

Now, loose-lipped as she was becoming, she still was veering as far away from the subject of the man as possible and was instead telling me further details that she felt were more important for my present and near future without her.

It seemed that her parents, dear Gram and Gramps, had wanted none of this business and had threatened to kick my mum out, if she didn't, er, get rid of the problem (i.e., me in her womb). Mum and Jem, close as they were, fought about it. Jem couldn't bear the thought of living with their smashingly jolly parents alone, so she begged Mum to do as they asked.

Poor woman had it coming at her from each and every side. And yet, here I am.

Growing up, I'd learned bits and pieces of all this. Very small bits. She'd kept it more or less under lock and key. It was obviously pretty painful for her, so at a certain age I'd learned to take the hint and stopped asking for the details. But now here they were, in nearly overwhelming number.

By this point in time as she lay dying, Gram and Gramps were dead or senile (can't say I remember which was which), so there was no getting them involved in the business—the business of my mother's death, that is. But Jem wasn't going to get off so easy.

Though the two of them had been quite out of touch in the years that followed my mother's "disgrace" (i.e., me), Mum had been able to piece together that Jem had married a wealthy American businessman and moved to the States at one point or another. And apparently there's nothing like impending death to break a grudge of years, because my mother actually rang her twin sister up. Now *that* was a doozy of a call. Especially the conclusion of it: "Say, now that I'm dying and all that, think you could take my son, the former cause of our decades-long separation, to live with you and your family, in your high-class American home?" I'm paraphrasing, of course. But that was her plan. And obviously, one can hardly refuse a dying sister.

Back to the present, then, as I sat by her deathbed, knowing that it was actually about the last of our alone moments together. For this now-infamous Aunt Jem was about to descend upon us in a matter of minutes.

"I do think it's more than possible that you'll end up loving it there and becoming smashingly happy," Mum was saying. Must be her drugs talking. I tried to muster an agreeing smile. But it was a task. "Promise me you'll try."

Deathbed and all, I could hardly refuse, as daunting a goal as it sounded. "Yes, Mum. Of course I'll try."

"You'll be off to university in less than a year, so you'll really only need to carry on with this arrangement a matter of months, you know."

"Yes Mum. I know. Please let's not waste time rehashing it. You've no need to worry about me."

She smiled. "You're right. Those American girls all have dreadful crushes on you dashing British men, so you'll have no choice but to make the most of it." My forced smile in return. "Okay, think I'll die now." And she closed her eyes.

I didn't bat an eye. She wasn't really dead. This was just her way.

She opened her eyes again. "No seriously, Calvin. Go find the priest so I can confess what a dreadful mum I've been to you and be on my way peacefully."

I leaned to kiss her on the forehead before leaving. "A lovely mum."

⸻

Well I did as she asked, and then found myself waiting outside the room during the confession, when this alleged aunt arrived.

I knew her immediately, even though the two of them

were very much not identical. Because their eyes were. Only, Aunt Jem's eyes were wrecked, saddened to their retinas, in contrast to my mum's, whose were distant but peaceful as she was basically just eager to be on her way to the next life by now.

This woman stopped a good three yards from me.

She stared at me. So I stared back.

And suddenly she burst into tears and threw her arms around my neck. I was taken aback briefly but quickly came to and started to give her little pats, a bit conscious of glances from onlookers.

"So sorry," she sniffed, trying to pull herself together. In a moment, there was no *trying* about it. She was a stiff stranger again. "I know you're Calvin. Obviously. Or I wouldn't have…" She made a vague gesture that was supposed to be indicative of her recent dissolvement into tears. "I stalked you on the internet. Isn't that what you kids call it?"

I cracked a small smile. "Quite so."

She glanced at the closed door. "Is she…?"

"Confessing."

She looked surprised. "Ah. Right. Makes sense, considering. Yes then." An awkward silence ensued. Until she pounced on it with, "You're seventeen? Just like my son, Josh."

I nodded. Something about this information struck me as strange, but only in that vague, indistinct way of something being buried under more important distractions. I could have given her some encouragement to keep talking, and maybe the point would have worked its way to the forefront of my mind, but I was hardly feeling like making the effort to behave in the outgoing way that usually came naturally to me.

Luckily the door opened just then to save me. Father Stone popped out, motioning us in. "We're through."

Auntie sighed relief. "Splendid." And strode inside.

She stopped cold at the sight of Mum, shrunken and . . . well, dying. "Jan!" Aunt Jem gasped.

My mum smiled weakly in response. "I don't mean to sound dramatic, but I do think you've made it just in time."

Aunt Jem hurried to her side, grabbed her outstretched hand.

And to my horror, the priest started saying something that I quickly realized were last rites.

I dropped to my knees beside her bed, reached desperately for her other hand, and realized I was too far away. Well that would hardly do. I scrambled up to change sides. My dying mother caught my eye as I did so, and I swear she nearly laughed at me through her agony.

Only her. Only the two of us could share a little joke at such a time. I nearly laughed back, but choked on it with a pang, as a feeling I'd never known washed over me.

That feeling was loneliness.

—

We stumbled through the next few days together somehow, Aunt Jem and I. Burial arrangements, funeral planning, the will. That last one should have been pretty simple—fairly broke, one heir. But it seemed my mother was actually in possession of a couple thousand pounds in savings at the time of her death, so I now had a bit of a college fund started. Didn't I feel privileged. If only I weren't about to embark on a journey halfway across the world to live with blood-strangers.

I cringed, noticing the bitter tone of my thoughts, the lack of gratitude. I could be out on the street alone, after all. Certainly that would be worse. Well, probably that would be worse.

I was musing these all-around pleasant thoughts as Aunt Jem and I finished up the last of the packing. Mum was in the ground, all the loose ends very nearly tied, and I was placing the last of my worldly belongings into my suitcase. My room, my former room that is, was bare. Aunt Jem had taken care of donating all the furniture and my mother's now-useless things during the intervening days. And we had a flight to catch in a couple hours.

I don't consider myself to be poetic, typically speaking. I've always been much more mathematically and scientifically inclined than toward anything imaginative. And yet, as I sat there in the emptiness, I couldn't help but think it symbolic. I felt as if my very heart might start to echo.

But I stood, ready to go. Because what my mum had wanted most, in her final days and really all her life, was my happiness. And she had sounded highly convinced that this was the surest route to that end. So I would do my darnedest, as these Americans might say, to honor her hopes by giving it my all.

"Quite through, then?" Aunt Jem was asking from the doorway.

"Yes. I guess so."

"Splendid. Cab's waiting."

I ignored the part of me that wanted desperately to linger a moment, say goodbye properly to the small room in the smaller apartment that had been my one and only home. No indeed, no time for threatening tears or fears. On my way, then.

The flight from London to Seattle, where Aunt Jem lived, was ten hours long. I armed myself with music and books, and I felt fairly confident that Aunt Jem wouldn't be busying herself about trying for some bonding moments between the two of us. If the death of a dearly loved one and its aftermath can't bond two people, I would venture to think that nothing can.

Well, I was venturing to think that nothing would, then, for Aunt Jem and me. Since that brief near-hysterical hug she'd given me in the hospital, it had been all business and distance between us. Considering what I assumed was some danger of those near-hysterics starting again if ever she were to crack a little in her demeanor, I'd tried to keep my emotional distance as well. So I was surprised when, getting settled into our seats on the plane (first class, compliments of Aunt Jem's rich husband), she closed her eyes, sighed, and said to me, "I've a feeling this will all work out for the best."

I glanced sharply at her, pausing to put in my ear buds. And I admit my first instinct was angry shock: "My mother is dead, you barely got to say goodbye to your estranged sister, I'm headed halfway across the world, and I don't bloody see how this could be anything but miserable for anyone involved, no matter what you or my dead mother might think!"

I said none of this, of course. I just mustered up a tight smile in response, a little nod maybe, and was about to carry on with the ear buds, when she went on. "I mean, of course you could always come back here to London for university in a few months, if you wanted. Surely this must be hard to leave your home."

I swallowed. The truth was I hardly felt like I had any

kind of home anymore, with my dear mum gone. I was leaving friends here, of course, but no one life-alteringly special. As much as it must paint me as a terrible mum's boy to say it, the woman truly was my best friend in life. So I suspected that coming back here for university in the fall would actually just be a piling-on of presumably somewhat healed pain.

She continued, "But you've also got us as family in the States now. Not to mention that that's actually where your father was from as well. So hopefully it can come to be a home to you eventually."

Come again? She'd said it like a throwaway line. Nothing of huge consequence. "I'm sorry, what was that? My father?"

She nodded. "He was an American university student in London for a study abroad. I thought you must have known."

I shook my head abruptly. No, I certainly had not known.

I managed another tight smile in attempt to sustain her friendly turn, but she seemed through with the topic and ready to get on with her own in-flight amusements, so I carried on with the ear buds. Lots for me to think about for the next ten hours, en route to the place where my story was about to begin and my life to change radically.

3

I DIDN'T KNOW IT yet at this point, but Sydney was the reason my life was about to change radically.

She hadn't the foggiest notion of what was getting started in her own life, either. It started innocuously enough.

"Sydney."

She heard her named called out behind her in the school hallway but thought she must have misheard. With Winnie off to her own classroom and nearly no one about, it seemed impossible that someone was calling to her, by name no less, rather than by insult. She did pause, briefly, and glance back. But upon seeing that the only ones around were some jocks, she internally shook her head and continued on.

"Hey, wait up. It's Sydney, right?" And footsteps approached.

So she glanced back again, an instant too slowly to see a look shared among them. Instead, all she saw was Josh

Simpson trotting toward her. Josh Simpson. Momentarily, she was confused. Because Josh Simpson was a guy upon whom, in some other reality where it wouldn't have been heartbreakingly pointless, she could have developed a crush. But in this reality, she would never have dared. Because Josh Simpson was essentially a god of everything at St. Aloysius: looks, popularity, athleticism, himself. So when she heard him calling to *her*, it could only mean one thing, and her spirits were about to plummet back to the depths of the terrible morning again, in certainty of further torments. But instead he surprised her: "Wanna go out with me Saturday night?"

Sydney stared at him in shock for a moment before her blush started and she stammered, "Me?"

He flashed a charming smile. "That's the idea. We'll see a movie or something. I think number ten in that one car chase franchise just came out, right?"

Never mind that watching number ten in that one car chase franchise was not Sydney's idea of a fun night. Never mind that at all. That thought was the smallest of tiny blips on her racing brain. Because a boy was asking her out, here in the middle of a student body where she'd only ever found one friend and had long ago given up on the idea of finding a boyfriend. And it wasn't just any boy. It was freaking Josh Simpson. It almost did not compute.

Almost. Because her romantic heart was firing on all cylinders. This was a girl who'd been dreaming of princes coming to her rescue since she was three. And while a guy asking a girl out to a movie might not sound too much like the romanticism of her dreams, it was so far beyond anything she had yet encountered in life that it thrilled her. In the approximately four seconds that elapsed before she answered, she couldn't help but think that finally, at long last, her happy ending was beginning.

So she smiled back, actually feeling for once that she might have as lovely a smile as her mother liked to attest. And she nodded. "Okay."

The bell was about to ring, and both knew it. "Awesome," he called, trotting backward toward his buddies and their classroom. "Wait, let me get your number." And he trotted back toward her, phone out.

Feeling still more than a little stunned, she quickly recited her number to him. And, without even realizing she was doing it, she analyzed him with her writer's brain and chalked up his forgetting to get her number to some kind of cute excitement on his own part. The thought made her relax a little.

And as she then carried on quickly to her own classroom, she dwelled on the amazed but exhilarated feeling, barely giving her natural doubt about *why* a second thought. Because she knew why, she just knew it. That finally, a guy really and truly liked her, and she was getting her chance at love and happiness.

—

For the first time in her academic life, Sydney found herself distracted in class and rather tempted to try and sneak a text to her best friend like any regular high school student. Of course she didn't, but the thought entered her mind.

And immediately upon seeing Winnie after class, she spilled her news in one breath. Winnie was amazed and excited for her, but did have to express aloud her confusion: "Holy crap, where did this come from?" Sydney shrugged back dramatically but couldn't keep the smile off her face. Until Winnie said, "Hey can I watch you break the news to your parents?"

Now Sydney sighed, shut her locker. "Been stealing candy from babies lately?"

Winnie laughed. "So can your mom like still do a cartwheel? Will she whip out the old pom-poms? Make up a cheer?"

"I think she will legitimately try to take a video."

"Watch, he'll lean in to kiss you, and surprise! There's Maryanne in the back seat."

"You are so not helping right now."

They started walking toward their calculus class. "What about your dad?" Winnie asked.

Sydney shook her head. "He'll say, 'Splendid. And how are his grades in physics? Will you and Josh be studying?'"

Winnie leaned in slyly and said in a faux-sexy voice, "Each other!"

Sydney shoved her, laughing but kind of uncomfortable. "Stop."

Winnie stopped, but said, "No seriously, just don't even tell them then."

"Would it be terrible if I told them I was going to your house and had him pick me up there?"

Sydney felt a twinge of guilt over the idea as she said it, but she immediately squelched it as Winnie said, "Dude, do it. Save yourself a world of hassle."

And so, Sydney proceeded with the plan to keep this first date from her parents, convinced it was not a big deal, rationalizing that her father certainly wouldn't care, and that her mother would make a much bigger deal of the matter than necessary. So instead, she focused on dealing with the more pressing matter with them: her play.

Actually, she would have much preferred that they not even know about that, either. But she knew this wouldn't be the case. There was little hope they would be in the dark about it for long, since Aunt Lisa had already sent her a congratulatory text.

As a fellow writer, Lisa had assumed, naturally, that it was spectacular news. Sydney's big break, so to speak. To Sydney, though, Lisa's well-meant text only seemed to mock her even further—how in the world had Aunt Lisa managed to hear about the play? Well, Aunt Lisa was a reporter. And it seemed that her paper was set to do a profile on the talented Sydney Camden.

Wouldn't that just make Sydney's classmates giddy.

While the looming date with Josh did definitely lessen the sting of impending ridicule, she was eager to get the bothersome conversation with her parents about her mockable achievement over with.

So that day after school, despite it's being Friday after-noon, Sydney took to her preferred manner of studying, out on her front lawn at home. The gray Seattle weather didn't always permit it, but this afternoon she was happy to see not a cloud in the sky. She brought her backpack full of things out, eager to pass the time until her parents got home. She was tempted to let her mind wander, but she said to her mind, *No!* and commanded it to channel her (very much alive) father, who was brilliant and intense in a rather abnormal measure. She often used thoughts of his brilliance as a sort of pep talk to herself when it came time to focus on school, particularly on the math- and science-based pursuits that came somewhat less instantly to her than the literary ones. But the truth was that the events of the day were very much inciting her heart toward her stories. So she sat cross-legged in her little nest of homework, with her notebook nearby for sudden bursts of inspiration.

About two and a half hours in to her nesting, if you will, a car pulled into the driveway. Sydney didn't look up, because she knew without doing so that it was only her hovering, perfect mother, arriving home right on schedule.

Maryanne Camden was one of those effervescent wonder-women who seemed quite able to do it all. She worked as a successful advertising executive, kept a picture-perfect home in a good neighborhood, had what appeared to be a top-notch marriage, and doted on her only daughter. All great news for Sydney. Especially when added to Maryanne's complete lack of awareness that Sydney often felt smothered.

Maryanne got out of her spotlessly clean high-end family sedan carrying an uncharacteristic bag of takeout.

"Oh my goodness! Sweetie! I heard the news! About your play!" she called to her daughter across the lawn.

Sydney suppressed a sigh and asked, "From Aunt Lisa?"

"No," her mom was saying as she juggled the food with some work materials and an empty coffee cup. "I heard about it from Kendall's dad. We just got an account with his company. So tell me everything, baby! This is so amazing! I even got takeout to celebrate." She waved the bag with much more exuberance than Sydney felt was called for. And went on: "What's your play called? What's it about? Are you gonna write a sequel?"

Sydney started gathering her books while trying to think of a way to avoid talking about her supposed accomplishment at all. But she was saved from answering by her dad pulling in.

Sydney's father Robert was of a different but also smashingly healthy parenting type. He was a thirty-eight-year-old nuclear physicist with high standards and what often seemed a total inability to emerge from his cold, scientific shell to show affection. To him, it was only natural that he should have a genius/prodigy as a child. It only baffled him as to why her field of excellence was so much more artistic in nature than his own.

The instant he emerged from his car: "Oh my goodness, Sydney, tell your father the exciting news!" from Maryanne.

"What news is this?" he asked in the sort of monotone that probably signified excitement. He glanced at the takeout. "Are we celebrating something?"

"Definitely! Tell him, Sydney."

Sydney reluctantly began, "Well I wrote this play for my English term project last semester—"

"And it's so good, they're performing it at school as the spring production!" her mother interrupted.

As they headed inside the house, Robert replied, "Very good. Promising news, Sydney."

Sydney paused on her way to the counter, glancing at her dad, maybe sort of hoping for a little more.

There was no more.

Robert went about removing his shoes, taking off his suit jacket, putting away his briefcase. Not even a congratulatory or approving glance toward his daughter.

So she crammed her feelings down deep inside where they seemed to belong, and she tried to laugh to herself at how closely his reaction mirrored her guess to Winnie earlier about what he'd say if she were to tell him about her date. And she set her books down, moving to join them at the table.

The three of them mumbled a quick, standard Catholic grace and began eating the Chinese. A rather stiff but typical affair. Except that Maryanne was still bubbling over with smothering excitement.

"So tell us more about it, Sydney."

What was there to tell? Certainly not the reactions of her peers to the news. Former high school cheerleader Maryanne was concerned enough knowing that Winnie was Sydney's only friend. No need to heighten her concern by providing any indication that Sydney's social life was much bleaker than her mother ever suspected.

In truth, Sydney was so eager to escape giving any hint about the reality of the situation that she actually considered changing the subject with news of her date. Certainly it would set her mother's mind at ease a bit, telling her that, oh look! Sydney might be able to find a boyfriend on her own after all.

Over the past couple years, Maryanne had been attempting, with supreme forced casualness, to get Sydney together with some nice young men who were sons of Maryanne's work friends. And the fact that Maryanne typically dropped the news of this teenage chap attending an evening's small dinner party along with his parents mere moments before the doorbell was rung did nothing to make it a pleasant experience for Sydney. Once the evening's events got going, the mixture of Sydney's nerves and inexperience, the fellow's general unwillingness to be there at all, and their bloody parents watching their every move, always brought the whole thing to exactly naught. Sydney didn't doubt that her mother's intentions were fine, great even. But what is it they say about good intentions? The road to hell and all that. Well, sometimes Sydney felt as if her mother's intentions were making her life rather hellish indeed.

So it was tempting just then to tell her mother triumphantly that a boy had asked her out. A cute, popular boy, in fact. And that—see?—she was plenty socially adjusted, not too focused on her writing, and doing just fine.

But Sydney couldn't do it. This date meant too much to her. She didn't want to chance ruining things or appearing sillier to Josh than he might already have thought her from her status at school, by having her freaking mother making a grand ta-do about the date. Eventually, Sydney reasoned, she would tell her mother, and her father too in case he cared. And she would put her mother at ease. But for now, Sydney was going to have to indulge her with information about her play, information that had nothing to do with the reaction of her classmates.

"Um, it's called *In the End*, and it's a romance that's a modern retelling of Shakespeare's *The Tempest,* told from the daughter Miranda's point of view."

"That's great, honey! What did everyone at school say?"

She quickly recounted some details about her English teacher's enthusiastic response and how the drama teacher loved it, talking as quickly as she could to prevent her mother from jumping in with more questions.

And then Sydney took an easy out by asking her father a question about physics. She was taking AP Physics this year solely for moments like this when she needed a diversion, and she was finding the class just challenging enough that she was able to ask him for help occasionally rather than take slightly longer to figure it out herself.

Thus, though she didn't know it, Sydney began setting herself up for circumstances that would prevent her from knowing just what do when things went terribly awry.

Everything went well, to start with. Through a careful act of timing coordination the next evening, Sydney and Winnie planned things so that Sydney would come over to her house after Winnie's mom left for her night-shift work, but would still have plenty of time in which Winnie could help Sydney with a bit of hair and makeup before Josh picked her up.

So far so good. Sydney's parents were none the wiser as she set out on her first real date with the most popular guy in school.

Now, Sydney really was a sensible girl. So she acknowledged to herself, as she sat in the theater for two hours of mindless action movie, that it was possible her expectations were too high. Because Josh was pleasant, fine, but not as breathtakingly, fantastically amazing a date as she had envisioned.

He'd made some small talk in the car, mostly about the school sports he excelled in, bought the tickets and popcorn, and then draped his arm around her by halfway through the previews. This obviously thrilled her a little, briefly. But eventually it got kind of uncomfortable, and she didn't quite know how to do anything about it.

Then, she thought perhaps at least this movie would turn out to be a fun experience with him. Whenever she and Winnie went to movies, they would talk and laugh, making fun and enjoying the film together, sometimes to the irritation of the other theater patrons. But all Josh did was watch, glued to the screen, and she found herself bored at crash, after chase sequence, after crash, after hot girl appearance.

Still, she remained optimistic about the drive back to

Winnie's. Before she knew it, she was on the porch with him, anxiously anticipating her first ever goodnight kiss.

But that anticipation didn't last long, because he was shoving his mouth onto hers immediately. She tried not to gasp, or breathe, or move. And she nearly died with relief as it ended, though she could hardly even admit it to herself. He was flashing his enchanting smile at her, saying something about having had a great time and he would call her. She nodded. And went inside.

She closed the door behind her, leaned against it, and saw Winnie's eager face.

"Details, woman! Speak!"

"Well…" Sydney began, plopping onto the couch.

"How amazing was it? I saw that kiss!"

Sydney cringed a little, certain she must have messed up the kiss somehow for it to have been so lame. And she delved into a detailed overview of the whole night for Winnie.

"Don't worry, first dates always suck," Winnie reassured her when she'd finished. "Just wait, second date will be perfect."

"You really think so?"

"I know so. How could it not be?"

Sydney was mildly reassured, though not entirely. The amazing love story of her dreams would not have begun with such little spark of connection. But she decided to take Winnie's advice and see what followed. This meant, though, that the cautionary part of her continued to hold off mentioning anything to her parents. If this was all to quickly come to nothing, she reasoned there was no point in dealing with what would probably be a lot of unpleasantness.

The weekend passed with no further contact from Josh, and she was beginning to think her misgivings about their belonging together were mutual. Monday morning dawned, and she was eager for school, hoping that if nothing else her uncertainty would be ended one way or another.

What she didn't expect was to find that the entire student body seemed to be staring at her. Apparently, news had spread that she had been on a date with Josh.

Beside her, Winnie was elated. But Sydney, despite the initial excitement, was worried. "What if it goes nowhere?" she whispered to Winnie.

"Worry, worry, worry. Come on, Syd. This could be amazing for you. Maybe you'll be popular now. I think it's about time you started pulling your social status weight in our friendship, because if we're being honest you've kind of been pulling me down for years…"

Sydney was only half listening, because she spotted Josh headed her way.

"Sydney. How's it going?"

She smiled in response, conscious that everyone was staring at them. She even noticed Kendall in her peripherals, starring daggers their way.

"Wanna come hang out with me and some friends tonight at Luigi's? We're gonna order like twenty pizzas and stake out that whole back room and maybe try to study for Collins's lit test if we get ambitious."

Sydney's eyes suddenly lit up. She really was a nerd to her core, because this sounded like a much more enjoyable evening to her.

So once again without letting her parents in on it, she went out with Josh. This time, she still felt awkward and very uncertain of how she felt about him, but she had a bunch of characteristic Sydney fun by explaining the first four chapters of *The Scarlet Letter* to a bunch of jocks. Now, some of these were the very people who often made massive fun of her, but she powered through her feelings of humiliation and bitterness, focusing on the fact that, for whatever reason right now, they were treating her like a human being. It was a lovely feeling, and so when Josh asked her out for a third date that weekend to kick off spring break, she agreed.

To her mind, all was well with the world. Because, in her innocence, she had no idea of what was lurking just beneath the surface of all this.

4

THAT WEEKEND on which her third date was to occur brings us to my arrival in the States with Aunt Jem, the doorway to my new life.

Aunt Jem brought me home from the airport, and in my jet-lagged, I'm-not-overwhelmed stupor, all I could really think about was how outlandishly large and high class this home of hers was. Mine. New home of mine. Correction. I shook my head at the impossibility, unable to imagine the day I would actually feel at home in this place.

We stepped inside, and my aunt relaxed visibly. She hung up her coat, and I could practically see the stress melting off her. Must be nice, I thought.

I stepped around her to take a look.

The house seemed just as high class on the inside as it had appeared outwardly, every convenience and luxury in the interior. Trendy art here, granite countertops there, everything inside matching the perfectly manicured lawn out front and the luxury sedan in the driveway. TVs in essentially every room, and more than enough space to prevent the awkwardness of being forced to have a social interaction with a fellow family member.

I felt my brow furrow—that wasn't fair of me to think like that before I even met them. There was quite the chance that Aunt Jem's family members weren't a bunch of entitled yuppies like their home seemed to suggest.

It was at this point in my musings that I first spotted my fifteen-year-old cousin, Pam. She sat in the living room, emotionlessly watching a slasher film. She was quite the picture of what Americans would call "emo."

In the den to the other side sat a man I could only presume to be my Uncle Sal. He was a handsome bloke, well built with a hint of approaching dad bod, but made to be rather worse looking by the scowl he wore as he sat in front of his fancy laptop. Fun fellow, I'm sure.

That's when I realized, to my shock, that Aunt Jem was actually crying quietly behind me. She saw my gaze and tried to hide it, but my mum's-boy instincts took over, and I dropped my bags to hold her again. Just like in the hospital.

Oh, the bloody hospital! And then here was I again, about to start the waterworks myself.

I was saved by the distraction of my other cousin entering. A teenaged boy near my own age. This was Josh. Yes, the very same Josh of Sydney's present-life events.

But I knew none of that just then. Rather, I was struck watching him trot lithely down the stairs into the kitchen, not a care in the world. I say *struck* because, of course, I was watching this over the shoulder of his sobbing mum.

He opened the fridge, started gulping milk out of a gallon jug, and then finally at long last seemed to notice us. But he pretended for another moment that he hadn't as he kept on drinking the milk.

He finally ventured an awkward glance toward his sobbing mother. But then he carried on ignoring her. He put the jug away and addressed me quietly, as if he were afraid of waking her or something: "Hey man, I'm off to practice. Uh, so I guess make yourself at home in my room and just don't touch my stuff."

He went ahead and slipped out the door past us, leaving me holding my crying aunt and thinking how bloody, fantastically easy it would be to fulfill my mother's dying hope and be happy here.

———

I've never thought of myself as materialistically spoiled. As a child of a single mother, I was used to a bit of scrimping and doing without.

But after setting eyes on this extravagant house, I was expecting that if nothing else good was to come of this terrible point in my life, at least being poor was over.

And then I learned that, as their spare space had been fashioned into such essential purposes as a weight room and a storage room, I was going to be sharing a room with Josh for the time being. Oh. I gulped, kind of cringing at my own disappointment. They were taking me in out of the goodness of their hearts, after all.

Never mind that Josh had not even come close to impressing me personality-wise in the forty-five seconds I'd seen him. And never mind that there'd now be no more or at least very little privacy for me to continue grieving the death of my mother. Never mind any of that. All was well here, I told myself. Because mum had hoped I'd be happy, so blast it all, I was going to be.

And then I saw the room.

The terms "swamp thing," "toxic waste," and perhaps "sewage treatment facility" came to mind.

The mounds of refuse that covered the floor were only absent, quite conspicuously, from a small circle that was cleared out for my new bed. A little foldaway cot.

"Just temporary," Aunt Jem was saying behind me. She stepped inside, kicking mounds of crap out of the way and off toward the side. "We'll go shopping for a real bed for you tomorrow maybe. Sorry about…" She was motioning toward the general refuse, as she did her best to do a super-quick tidy job.

I quickly shook my head. "No, don't worry about it. I'm not fancy. Don't bother." She sighed, gave me an apprecia-tive glance, and with a nod, left me to it.

My eyes automatically followed her toward the door, but then I nearly jumped. Because staring back at me from right above my little cot were eyes. Eyes on a poster. These eyes were about the only place I felt comfortable looking. They belonged to a surgically enhanced, miniature bikini-clad woman.

I glanced around at the refuse and located a crumpled dirty T-shirt. It kind of reeked, but I picked it up anyway. "Sorry for the stench, love," I apologized to her as I used the poster's tacks to arrange the shirt on the wall over her near-naked body. "But at least you won't be so cold now, hmm?" And I sat down on the cot, glancing up behind myself at my only company. "Guess it's just you and me."

And that's when the laughter started.

It seemed such a joke. All of it. I laughed, and I laughed some more, somehow certain my mum was laughing along with me, up in Heaven. She and Jesus were having a smashing good time watching, as I settled in to my new home, feeling closer to the poor sort-of porn star on the wall than to most of my supposed family members.

And suddenly energized with a strange feeling of closeness to my mum, as if somehow my absurd laughter was the start of her fulfilled hope, I resolved to burrow in and set about unpacking for my new life.

—

The next morning, my first morning in America, I awoke at a frightening hour. Thank you, jet lag. I was bit disoriented, and as I started to get my bearings I decided I was glad I was not the type of person to go out on a drinking bender, because this not-knowing-where-you-are business is a very unpleasant one. Though of course in my present circumstances, it was even more unpleasant because life in general was so right now.

Across from me in the dim around-dawn light, I could see Josh's dead-asleep form and decided he was not likely to awaken if I got up this early. So I tiptoed downstairs, discovering that no one was stirring in the house.

It all felt vaguely intrusive, like I wasn't supposed to be here, and I didn't quite know what to do with myself. Eventually I settled on the telly, glancing over my shoulder every few moments as if someone might catch me, while I watched some ridiculous children's programming for lack of better options.

Finally, by half-past seven, I decided no one of them could really plan to sleep that much longer anyway, and so I quit with the telly and began some breakfast preparations. Might as well make myself agreeable and whip up something delicious for everyone.

But alas, several eggs and some improvised pancakes later,

no one had yet made an appearance, nor was there even a sign of life. I ate my breakfast in solitude and wrapped the rest in foil with a note, "Help yourself."

I went back upstairs and began a leisurely morning routine—shower, shave, and all that—Josh still not stirring. One might think him legitimately dead, he was so still. And then, the rest of the house *still* unearthly quiet, I gave up on the time-wasting and the hope that Aunt Jem would be up soon to go "real bed" shopping, and I went out to explore the city myself.

I'd very much been counting on a bit of time with dear Aunt today, as I was hoping to ply her for more information concerning my illusive father. A name, at the very least. Obviously, America is large country, but having a name might certainly help if I got up the nerve to track him down.

But instead of beginning on anything so productive as that, I found myself wandering about Seattle for the day, feeling as alone as ever as I merged with the swarms of people.

The city was not so very different from London or any other big city, really. I found that my new family lived in an almost quaint suburb, with some little streets here and some housing developments there, cookie-cutter upscale homes with the Space Needle looming off in the background. And down the street not far was St. Aloysius Academy, my new school.

I rode the bus a bit, took in some sights, began counting the abundant collection of coffee shops, and all the while was beginning to dream about this unknown fellow, my father, wondering such things as how he took his coffee, and whether the intervening years might have perhaps healed the grudge he bore toward my existence, as had seemed to be the case with Aunt Jem. A part of me knew it might be foolish or unrealistic, yet I couldn't help but hope that perhaps finding him and, you know, forming some kind of corny American '50s sitcom father-son connection with him might be a part of my "all work out for the best" story here. A fellow needed a family, after all.

I was finally jostled out of these thoughts at the sight of a used bicycle store. A perfect answer to my current lack of transportation.

I purchased a possibly overpriced (conversion rate was getting me) but only gently used mountain bike and decided to ride it back.

That was when I saw them. I was nearly back to that little high-class suburb area of my new so-called home when I passed some kind of medical building with a sign titled Women's Health. I would have given it very little thought but for the fact that there were nearly a dozen people standing in front of it, holding various signs and pamphlets. I pulled to a stop, curiosity getting the better of me.

A sweet-looking curly-haired old lady smiled and waved at me. "Hello there, dear." I smiled back as I scanned their signs, caught sight of the rosaries, noticed the security guard watching warily from the entrance.

Another time, perhaps I would have made a full stop, had a conversation, fallen in with them, even. But just then, all I could think about was Mum. And her hard, short life, filled with caring for her much-loved little son, with utter desertion from her family but not an ounce of personal regret. And, as much as I wished I could have honored her memory by joining in with something she would have approved quite heartily of, I instead found myself doing just the opposite of what she would have probably liked, tearing up and riding off in a cloud of grief.

By that evening, I wish I could say that my day had improved considerably. But I found myself sitting alone on that pitiful cot, in pajama pants and a T-shirt, eating leftover stew that had probably always been leftover as no one was ever seen eating together in this house, with only the newly clad wall porn star behind me for company.

And if that weren't dismal enough, my meal was accompanied by the lovely sound of Aunt Jem and Uncle Sal having a passive-aggressive fight-like discussion.

"No one is going to sue us, Jem. You don't need to nag at me. I know what I'm doing," Uncle Sal was saying in a stern tone.

"Can't say that sounds terribly different from what you said last time, when they *did* try to sue us," Aunt Jem said in a rising tone that was still not an obvious, full-on fight.

This was followed by the sound of Pam slamming her bedroom door down the hall from me and then blasting her grunge music. Ah, my new happy family. I gathered, from the continuation of the non-fight that followed, that Uncle Sal was perhaps not the most aboveboard businessman, and that his company had been sued once already because of his practices. I listened to this go on for several cringe-worthy minutes, their pissed voices seeming to emphasize just how un-home-like this entire situation was.

And yet, I can't say that all this rot suddenly heaped onto my life was truly terrible. Painful, sure. Bothersome, absolutely. But I didn't know truly terrible until I met Sydney and discovered her story.

5

THIS THIRD DATE of Sydney's began with nothing suspicious. She had Josh pick her up at Winnie's once again, reasoning that if this night was as enjoyable as the evening she'd spent with him and his less attractive friends, she would soon bite the bullet and tell her parents.

He took her to dinner at a nice-ish Italian chain restaurant. She first ate delicious breadsticks, then internally kicked herself over not bringing gum for the inevitable garlic breath, and . . . immediately noticed him checking out their waitress's bum. Sydney's spirits fell a bit at that. But in her optimistic inexperience, she thought perhaps she'd seen it wrong, or even that maybe he had some bad habits he was trying to break. And now that their order was placed, they would actually have some time for real conversation alone. She forced her nerves to calm and smiled tentatively at him . . . as he looked completely past her at the game on TV in the bar.

All in all, it was not even close to the lovely evening she had been anticipating. She tried to stem the tide of disappointment as he paid the bill and made small talk about some sports team she was completely unfamiliar with. They got in his car, and she wasn't sure how to feel. She wanted *so* badly for this all to be amazing, but it just wasn't.

And it was strange to her that Josh didn't seem to notice this. He was carrying on with his brilliant smiles and saying something about the night being young as he turned down a street in the opposite direction of Winnie's house.

Sydney sat up straighter. "Where are we going?" Maybe he had some genius and thoughtful activity planned for the rest of the evening.

He smirked. "You'll see. I've got the inside intel. We're getting the good stuff."

"What good stuff?"

In answer, he pulled in to a liquor store.

Her face fell. And her stomach dropped. The only drinking she'd ever done was the half-glass of wine her parents let her have at major holiday dinners. She and Winnie had joked in the past, during their occasional sleepovers at Winnie's house, that they should break into her mother's cabinet of goods and have themselves a real night of it. But they never did, between Winnie's fear of being caught and Sydney's residual, innate good-girl elements.

And now, here was a guy about to buy her some alchie.

He opened his door and got out. "You coming?"

Of course he would expect her to come in. Why hadn't she moved yet? She gulped and nodded, getting out.

The following four and a half minutes demonstrated to Sydney just how easy it actually was to get away with things when you're a confident guy used to getting his way. The clerk didn't ask for ID and barely even looked twice as Josh purchased a bottle of caramel-flavored vodka.

Josh lead the way back to the car, smirking and just about oozing arrogance. Sydney was a little bit alarmed to see him open the bottle and take a large swig as he got back into the driver's seat. And he offered the bottle to her.

"Uh…"

Her mind was a-fritz with alarm bells and warning signals. But really, a lifetime of near-social solitude and of parental guidance that consisted of either academic training or of pushing toward whatever was typical for a teenager did little to prepare her for this moment.

She took a drink.

She knew it was a terrible idea, and even as she swallowed she was regretting it. Josh, of course, did not notice this. "Good stuff, huh? You girls always go for the caramel one."

Sydney could feel the vodka stinging its way down into her stomach, and she imagined it entering her bloodstream at what was probably a much faster rate than in reality. And yet, the significance of the phrase he had just uttered hit her mind with alarming clarity. She turned and stared at the guy. Just how many girls had he bought caramel-flavored vodka for? And to what end?

Her stomach dropped again as he began driving, still not in the direction of Winnie's house. Her mind filled with all those warnings she'd ever heard against drunk driving, wondering how impaired Josh was from the large drink he'd taken. But she was even more preoccupied with the realization of what she had been denying and hoping against: Josh was not her prince charming. Not even close.

She wanted to strongly and confidently tell him so, express out loud to this guy just how disappointed she was, demand to know what his motives were in asking her out in the first place. But she didn't trust herself. She was suddenly becoming too frazzled with thoughts of possible answers to that question. So all that came out was a quiet, "Take me home?"

He glanced at her, shook his head with a dazzling smile. "It's still early. I've got a much better idea."

He was pulling into the deserted parking lot of a community park. Families and kids had left for the night. Sydney's heart quickened, but she forced herself to remain calm, tried to think through the mild fog from the booze. She suspected her hands were shaking, but she put all her strength into making her voice level as she said, "I want to go home."

He ignored this and put the car in park. Turned off the engine. And opened the bottle again, offering it to her. She shook her head no. He frowned at this. "You had a good time tonight, right?"

"Um…"

"I kind of like to think I know how to treat a girl right…" He was turning to face her, getting too close, and very sure of what he was after.

Sydney was just as sure of what she didn't want to happen. But in the end, that didn't seem to matter.

A time would come when I would learn about all this, to my absolute horror. But for now, I was just an unconnected piece of the story, sitting in Josh's pigsty of a room alone and struggling with the fact that I currently liked nothing about most of these family members or their home. And each new point to the argument between my aunt and uncle seemed to punctuate all this.

Finally, by about ten thirty, I really couldn't take being in that house for another second and found myself trotting down the stairs in my pj's and running shoes. And I unfortunately couldn't escape passing Aunt Jem and Uncle Sal's continuing discussion in the den.

They stopped with an almost comical abruptness as I passed them. "Eh, headed out for a little jog," I offered. They glanced at the clock, and back at me a little strangely. "Don't mind me. Carry on. Maybe…" I wanted to say they should try yelling and get it all out, but I decided in favor of keeping my nose out of their marital problems. "I'll just…" And I saw myself out.

Once out, I breathed. And spontaneously broke into a sprint.

The thing is, I couldn't have known it, but as I ran one direction on that little suburb street, Sydney was walking just a street over. Walking now, finally through with the run she'd started out at. Distressed. Haunted. Sickened at what she had just undergone.

But I didn't know any of this as I ran, fueled by frustration, grief, anger, confusion, helplessness. I was oblivious. To everything, as a matter of fact, for a car was following me. A sedan, with lots of antennas. I couldn't be bothered to glance at it.

Until it pulled up right beside me, window down. The person inside addressed me thus: "Hey kid, why are you out here running at this hour? In pajama pants?"

To which I glibly replied, "Would you prefer I'd have skipped the pants altogether? Bugger off and let a man blow his steam, will you?"

That's when I finally glanced over at this new friend. And saw he was a copper. A young, extra-angry one. Catching one look at that face, I ceremoniously dubbed him "Frownie Cop." And I decided I had probably better come to a halt.

"Sorry," I said through my labored breathing. "Didn't realize you were a copper. Or so frownie. Am I breaking a law or something? Do apologize . . . just arrived here . . . across the pond, you know . . ."

"No law," he was saying, "I just don't like the look of you. Or your pants, if I'm being honest."

"Maybe don't be honest?" I couldn't help but quip back.

His radio crackled. "Motor vehicle crash, head-on collision, Fifth and Pine."

He sighed and gave me one last stink eye. "I've got my eye on you, Brit."

He rolled up his window and sped off, leaving me waving after him. "Lovely chatting with you too, my ill-tempered friend!"

And, between the endorphins of the run and the innate humor of the situation with this spectacularly pissy cop, I once again found myself in better spirits. I couldn't help but laugh, shaking my head and wondering what on earth my mother was praying for, for me from up there.

Sydney, meanwhile, was having no such promising turn to her evening.

She had finally reached the theoretical comfort of Winnie's house once again, but after choking out a brief recap of what had happened, all Sydney could do was sit shaking on the couch while Winnie rummaged in the kitchen.

"Maybe chocolate?" Winnie was asking her. "Some ice cream? Or how about a shot? I'll totally break into mom's cabinet tonight if you want. I think the situation might call for some tequila or something . . ."

Sydney looked up in alarm, sputtering at her friend's cluelessness. "No. Don't you—I don't want . . ." She barely knew how to formulate words to express how far from an appropriate response this felt.

"Might help take the edge off," Winnie popped back in to offer. Sydney only shot her a look of death in reply. "Holy crap, okay, sorry. Chocolate it is." And Winnie grabbed a ridiculous-sized slab of chocolate for their munching purposes.

Sydney nervously took a piece, hands still shaking, mind unable to catch up with the ridiculousness of eating chocolate at a time like this. Instead, she was rapidly trying to understand. "I'm an idiot, aren't I?" she had to ask.

"Noooo . . ."

"What's that mean?"

"It means . . . Okay, look. We both know you're not on the upper end of the food chain. It was obviously fishy that he wanted to go out with you."

What Sydney had been piecing together was making more and more sense, as the chocolate actually helped to calm her nerves. "He thought I'd be an easy lay." Winnie nodded sagely. "You should have told me," Sydney accused.

"Told you what? I mean, Syd come on. Just look at the guy. I know you've got your good-girl thing going on, but I thought you might be into it. I mean I'd tap that."

Ninety-nine percent of the time these two had known each other, they'd been very much on the same page, in strangely perfect sync with one another when it came to matters of both personality and preferences. But that other one percent of the time, nearly all of which had been during this school year, Sydney was jolted by just how different the two of them could be.

This evening definitely fell into that one percent. Sydney was considering just springing up and leaving. Wading through this unexpected turmoil all alone would certainly beat hearing things like this from her best friend right now.

But then Winnie stepped up in the good sense department and said, "But he seriously crossed a line. No means no, jackass, and he should rot in hell."

Winnie cursed him some more, in much cruder terms than Sydney would have necessarily used, but the feeling behind the words was a complete match to Sydney's shattered heart. The very sound flowed into Sydney's wounds and began to soothe them. And it opened the floodgates.

The tears came, and Winnie held her like a best friend should, until Sydney's tear ducts finally, at long last, began to settle down.

"Okay. Okay," Sydney was saying, ready to collect herself again. Or try to, anyway. At first she could only choke out, "What do I do now? What do I do?"

"Um, what *can* you do? I mean, do you want to call the cops?"

"Is that . . . that's what you do, right?" Sydney held her head, trying to think through the numb haze she was feeling. What she really wanted right now was her notebook. She wanted to write. Escape into a much more pleasant world. But she had to figure this out. There was no hiding. Not yet.

"Honestly, I'm not sure," Winnie said. "Okay let's think about this. Everyone knew you were sort of dating a little, I think. I heard Kendall was jealie, so probably everyone knows *something* about it. And we know no one is really crazy about you. I mean, what, you press charges, get him locked away, and the whole school hates you. More than usual, right? And like, you *were* dating. It won't be hard for him to say you wanted it . . ."

The terribleness of what Winnie was saying sank in. "And who's gonna believe the freaky nerd girl they laugh at for fun? When he says . . . says . . ."

Winnie gave her a shrug that said, *It is what it is.* Which almost brought new tears to Sydney's eyes.

Nope. Not happening.

"Get me some paper and a pen," she demanded.

Winnie was momentarily puzzled before rolling her eyes and complying. Typical Sydney. "You need to make a pro/ con list or something?"

Sydney shook her head no and eagerly took the pen and paper from her friend. She paused a moment, collecting her thoughts, and dove in: *On the night of April second, at approximately nine-thirty p.m., Joshua Simpson died a slow and painful death resulting from injuries he obtained in a fiery head-on collision. As he was not wearing his seat belt, the force of the collision sent him through the windshield, where he skidded across the pavement, leading to his bloody, gruesome demise.*

Winnie read it over her shoulder. "That's perfect. Does it make you feel better?"

Sydney nodded. A lie. She still felt terribly, abominably shitty.

But she had to try to believe that allowing herself to hate him and that even fantasizing about his death—contrary to the whole love-is-good-hate-is-bad-you-probably-shouldn't-wish-death-on-anyone way she had been raised—would do *something* to make her feel better. So she held on tight to that mental picture of Josh dying and tried to let it comfort her, having no idea that, very soon, it would break her.

$$6$$

I'VE HEARD IT SAID BEFORE that Catholics shouldn't believe in coincidences. And I think that's more or less accurate when you break it down. So even though it might have seemed like an outrageous coincidence that Sydney dreamed up that car crash for Josh at that particular point in time, it wasn't. She might not have been consciously thinking of the fact that he was speeding away somewhat nervously from their encounter, on a few shots of vodka nonetheless; but she was rather a master at plotting, so it probably wasn't a hard one to figure out, as much as she never dreamed her literary endeavor would be accurate. But, spoiler, it was strangely so. Remember Frownie Cop's radio crackle, as he left me? The news of a head-on collision? That head-on collision was in fact the result of Josh speeding through a red light and hitting a car turning toward him, a short time before Sydney dreamed up something very similar.

I've often pondered just why all this had to happen on the same night. And ultimately, I still do not think it a coincidence but rather the catalyst for a series of terrible events that did eventually work for the good of us all. Except for Josh, it would almost seem. Almost.

Questions of coincidence aside, my second night in America was a strange and tragic one indeed, one in which I was awakened from already disorienting time-difference sleep to the sound of wailing and sobbing, to the sight of frantic grabs for jacket and shoes, as the family almost forgot about me in their dash to the car. I hurried to hop in anyway, my stupor fading away as we sped toward the hospital.

I couldn't help but think about what a bizarre way this was to start a new life for myself. My mother dies, and I head to a new country to settle in with a new supposed-family for all of a day and a half, and everything goes to crap for them as well, in the way of unexpected deaths anyway? Was the grim reaper himself following me about?

Things were a mess at the hospital. All of it was one big terrible mess. Josh was in very bad shape, slipping in and out of consciousness and too unstable for the doctors to do much. As there was a limit to visitors, I mostly hovered in the hallway, letting his mum, dad, and sister have their time alone with him. I peaked in now and then, and at one point saw him struggling to whisper something into Pam's ear, but I thought little of it. All I knew was that he was in dire shape, that much was clear. And truth be told, I didn't know how to deal with it just then.

But if nothing else, at least this unimaginable misery of theirs seemed pretty clear-cut. Quite unlike the confusing turmoil that was about to be thrown at Sydney.

At the end of that terrible evening, Winnie dropped Sydney off at home near her curfew time, and Sydney's parents were just heading to bed themselves. She did her best to zoom past them to her room, and they didn't notice anything amiss, of course having no reason to suspect that she had undergone anything other than a night of hanging out with Winnie.

Once alone in her room, Sydney tried to collect her thoughts. Which she quickly decided was a terrible idea. She wanted absolutely nothing to do with thoughts of her evening. Sleep sounded good, but she suspected it would be fairly impossible. What she really wanted was a shower. A second shower, in fact, as Winnie had already let her take one at her house. Yet one shower hardly felt sufficient to make Sydney close to comfortable or clean again. But she suspected it would raise red flags with her mother if she did it right now, so she decided she needed to kill about forty-five minutes to be sure her parents would be asleep.

She looked to her book collection. And quickly gave up on the idea of reading—no need to ruin a perfectly good book with associations of this wretched night. She wanted to write, *needed* to write, but she was afraid of what exactly would try to make its way out of her pen tonight. Certainly nothing that could be contained to the next forty-five minutes. So instead she settled on cleaning her room. First item on the list: take down the '90s boy-band poster Winnie had given her as a joke. Because right now, she felt like these charming young fellows were staring at her lustfully. No good. Down it came.

She spent the next half hour straightening, sorting, dusting, taking a minuscule amount of comfort from the order she was restoring. And then finally she got to her shower.

She imagined she was washing Josh off her, cleaning off how dirty and soiled she still felt. And she tried to dwell on the feeling of cleanliness when she was done. But it didn't last.

By about two a.m., she was sitting cross-legged in her bed, deep in the process of trying to write something, anything, that would make her feel better. A pretty fruitless endeavor.

An hour later found her no nearer sleep and in an unchanged position, only now she had added a childhood stuffed bunny into the crook of her arm as she wrote.

By five, she was still at it, but making no better progress. She'd given up on the story she had been working on pre–terrible night, or had given it up in essence anyway, because now things were taking an entirely different direction: *Despite having absurdly frizzy hair, the girl enjoyed a blissful life, free of tragedy or attacks of any kind. Until…*

Nope. She angrily crossed it all out and suppressed the urge to hurl the notebook across the room.

Sighing, she rearranged herself and glanced at the bunny. Looked at him suspiciously as her weariness kicked in. "What?" she asked him. She shook her head and shoved the bunny down under her bed.

She caught sight of her phone on the nightstand and stared at it. She could try, if only she were a smidgen braver, to call her Aunt Lisa. If there were a person in the world she *might* consider talking to about this, it would be her.

But to tell anyone, for anyone else to know … it would probably be the start of many further unpleasant things. First, telling her parents how she had deceived them— perhaps the least of her worries. The big issue in her mind was that she could only imagine how reporting him would serve to prolong all this misery. Right now, she felt like her best hope of ever feeling normal again was to try her hardest to forget and to somehow avoid seeing him again for the remaining two and a half months of school.

No. With decision, Sydney turned her gaze away from her phone and decided against calling Aunt Lisa or telling anyone ever.

And that was when her phone rang. She all but jumped right off the bed at the sound. *Buzz, buzz.* Slowly, she reached for it, half-expecting it to uncannily be her aunt. Instead, she read a number she had never seen before.

She shot a glance around the room, as if there might be someone to advise her what to do, because she knew in her gut that nothing good was going to come from whatever this phone call might be.

She hesitantly picked the phone up off the nightstand, and her fingers hovered over the answer button a moment before she gulped and pressed it.

She held the phone to her ear like any normal person but forgot to say anything.

"Hello?" a female voice said after a moment. "Hello? Is this Sydney?"

Sydney found herself nodding. Realizing her absurdity, she swallowed and murmured, "Mmm hmm."

The voice on the phone continued, "This is Pam Simpson, Josh's sister. He … he told me what he …" A pause, agony for Sydney's frantically spinning mind. "He just died from a car crash." A beat, as if the girl were waiting for Sydney to respond. But of course she didn't. She was too joltingly stunned. So Pam said, "I just thought you should know." And hung up. *Click.*

Sydney could do nothing but stare at her phone for a moment, unable to fully process. But as the meaning of the words sank in, her eyes roved toward her notebook. Toward the scene she had written. Absolutely horrified.

And so, Sydney began to bloody well lose it.

—

The morning found Sydney in pretty rough shape, eyes bloodshot and nearly shaking with exhaustion. Post–phone call, she had wrestled the remainder of the early morning hours with the question of whether she had somehow caused Josh's accident by dreaming it up. Logic told her no. Righteous anger told her hopefully. Guilt told her hopefully not. The end result was no sleep and pure misery.

And now she had to figure out how to try and look somewhat normal in front of her parents.

She tried to avoid them as much as possible, hide in a book as they ate breakfast, keep her face blank, control her shaking hands and go about her Sunday morning as usual. But by the time the three of them were in the car on the way to 10:30 Mass like the perfect Catholic family that they weren't, she couldn't take it anymore.

She was plugging away and trying her best to keep her misery off her face, but the law of probability dictated that her mother could only go so long without noticing. "Sydney? Are you okay, honey? Is something wrong?" Maryanne asked as they neared the church parking lot.

Sydney had expected the questions to come eventually but

still felt ill-prepared. "Um…" Buying time. She had to tell them something, or she might just burst. Especially knowing that Maryanne would be a bulldog about getting some truth out of her. "I got a phone call early this morning…"

Now both parents glanced back at the sound of tears in her voice. Might as well sell it, the half of it she was telling. "A guy from school, um, got in a car crash last night?"

Maryanne exclaimed, "Oh no! Is he okay?" Sydney only shook her head in response. Maryanne ventured, "What happened?"

"He—he died."

Even Robert nearly gasped. Maryanne hurried to ask, "Did you know him?"

Sydney nodded. "We… hung out a couple times?" No need to go into too many details, now that there were some very solid reasons to be sure the relationship was not going to go anywhere (him being a dead rapist and all).

"Oh, sweetie!" And Maryanne was all comfort as they pulled in to the church parking lot. She was unbuckling, reaching back, but Sydney shrank away, uncomfortable with the sympathy under false pretenses. She wasn't crying over his being dead, after all. She shook her head, wiping her eyes. "I'd rather not look like a mess. I'm fine. Just…" She swiped at her snot and tears and got out of the car.

Maryanne's concerned gaze followed her, but her parents didn't immediately follow her out. She saw them tersely discussing her for a moment, and though she couldn't hear them, she knew with certainty what they were assuming: that she had told them the whole truth. The fact that she hadn't made her feel a little rotten. But certainly, she assured herself, not as rotten as she'd feel if she had had to relive last night by recounting it.

ON MY PART, I had a bit of an unusual Sunday myself, to
put it lightly. I ended up tracking down an evening Mass at
one of the many Seattle Catholic churches, and I attended
alone. Such practices seemed the furthest thing possible
from the minds of my new grieving family members,
and most likely not just because they were otherwise
preoccupied. It seemed that St. Aloysius Academy was only
important to them for its prestige, rather than any benefits
of religious instruction.

In the days immediately following all this, things
remained predictably desolate. I quickly discovered that
superstar Josh had been his shallow father's pride and joy,
his already grieving mother's baby boy, and his sister's . . .
something. Pam's behavior rather puzzled me. She seemed
much angrier than the typical grieving sister, but for the
time being I wrote it off as just the only way her emo-ness
would let her express the grief, and I continued trying
to make it clear to her that I was there and available for
anything she might need. Of course she needed nothing.

All in all, my feelings of awkwardness didn't soon decrease. Especially considering that here I was, living in the guy's room, his dirty clothes and random filth threatening to attack me, and yet he had gone and died before I'd had the chance to speak a word to him. But if I were being really honest, the reason I felt most awkward was that I had quickly decided I didn't like him one bit before even giving him much of a chance—and now he was dead. I tried to ignore the twinge of guilt and focused my energy on doing what I could to help the rest of the family throughout that following long and empty spring break week holiday.

I found that any efforts I made to be of use or comfort were met with stony rejection by Uncle Sal, some appreciation but certainly further weeping by Aunt Jem, and angry stares from Pam. And so I kept rather to myself, fighting the overwhelmingness of the grief over my mother that threatened to engulf me every time I dared contemplate the wretchedness of my existence here.

But one could hardly look forward to the end of this spring break, because it was to bring more fun: Josh's funeral.

Being as he was such a bloody school hero and all, about the only place big enough to hold all his heartbroken friends and admirers was the St. Aloysius school gym. I briefly allowed myself a sliver of anticipation over seeing what was to be my new school for the last two and a half months of the term. But very briefly. We were heading to a funeral, after all. I could only hope it would be the last I'd have to attend until I was so old that my acquaintances started dropping of natural old age causes.

As for Sydney, she was attending as well. It seemed that she had to. The school had gotten right on the task of notifying all parents of the situation, along with encouraging parents to talk to their children about it, be there for them, offer grief counseling … All of which Maryanne quite readily did.

Sydney tried to act naturally about it, but she couldn't emphasize enough that she did not need grief counseling, as she suspected a professional would probably get the horrible truth right out of her. But Maryanne, as distraught as she was over the whole situation in which her near-hermit daughter finally seemed to like a boy who then promptly croaked, did suspect that Sydney seemed to be grieving properly. As evidenced by the fact that Sydney spent a good amount of the spring break hanging out alone in her room, followed by brief periods of residual blotchy face, the kind that Maryanne quickly and accurately associated with weeping.

Her parents naturally assumed she would be attending Josh's funeral, knowing of no reason why she should not be interested in celebrating his life and praying for his soul. So Sydney braced herself, tried her best to dive deep into the relieving numbness she was occasionally able to find, and went along with them to the gym that next Friday afternoon.

Winnie spotted her immediately in the parking lot. "She lives!" Winnie said, pulling Sydney a little away from her parents and discreetly doing a little dance.

"What the hell are you doing?"

"Partying, now that he's dead. I figured that must be what you've been up to all week. Why haven't you called me?" Sydney only shrugged in response, starting to feel a little self-conscious. It seemed a bit as though she was being stared at as they made their way inside to find seats in the bleachers. She tried to ignore the feeling and told herself it was her imagination.

It wasn't her imagination.

Not a moment after they sat, with her nerves already on edge, she was startled to feel a hand on her shoulder and jumped with a fright far out of proportion to the situation. If she'd been thinking as analytically as she was wont to do in her moments of writing genius, she might have noticed that there was no good reason to jump like that just then. But analytical thinking was nowhere in sight. Only panic was, panic at an unexpected and unwelcome touch. She snapped her head around to see whose hand was encroaching into the bubble of her shoulder, and she found it belonging to this gangly freshman nerdy guy.

He pulled his hand back quickly. "Sorry," he said. "Didn't mean to startle you, Sydney. I just wanted to say sorry about Josh. Are you doing okay?"

She looked at him blankly for a moment, conscious of her mother pretending not to watch beside her, and of Winnie not even pretending on the other side. And Sydney's stomach plummeted, her face hardened, even as she fought through the responses forming in her mind. Because she knew what was about to happen and very much did not want her mother to see it. She waited for it, for him to go on, for the punch line that made her the butt to his joke, to all their jokes.

But the guy only stared back, blinked, and waited dumbly for her to respond.

And here is where Winnie stepped in. She slipped an arm around Sydney and said, "She's hanging in there. A little overwhelmed." This seemed to satisfy the guy, and he went on his way.

Maryanne reached a comforting hand over to pat Sydney on the knee, quite thoroughly buying Winnie's excuse herself.

Winnie shot a questioning glance toward Sydney, as if to say, **What the hell, lady?** in reference to her frozen non-response.

Sydney, understanding the silent question perfectly, responded with a shrug and whispered, "Just waiting for the usual."

But even as she whispered it, a group of mildly popular girls was headed their way.

"You know, something tells me your usual is about to change." Occasionally, Winnie came up with an accurate insight on life situations at hand. This was one of those rare occasions.

Because sure enough, one of the girls came right up to Sydney and said, "It's Sydney, right? You're so strong. I can't imagine what you're going through." And then, to Sydney's astonishment, this random girl hugged her! Sydney's shock was so great that it only barely registered in her mind that this hug was less offensive to her senses than Nerd Boy's shoulder touch. Matters to be pondered later, to be sure, but right now she had to focus on the task of faking her way through a return hug to a girl who had probably laughed at jokes about her countless times.

And, that accomplished with a passable grade in social skill, the group of girls moved on, and Maryanne reached to give Sydney another little squeeze, pleased for Sydney's sake.

But Sydney could hardly wrap her mind around what seemed to be going on. She merely shook her head in bewilderment at Winnie, who leaned over and whispered, "Dude, don't even question it. You have *got* to roll with this."

Sydney kind of nodded, wanting to agree. Hadn't she always wanted her craptacular social status to improve? But she couldn't quite pretend that it sat one hundred per cent right with her.

Nonetheless, there was nothing to do about it now. Now was reserved specifically for turning off all thought and emotion as much as possible, for the funeral of her rapist was about to start.

———

I sat through that funeral down in the front row with my new, ripped-apart family, all the awkwardness of the past few days tripled as I felt like some extra, impostor type. "Who is that random fellow with Josh's family?" everyone must be asking. "He looks about the same age. Did they get a replacement boy?"

As for the family themselves, Aunt Jem was openly weeping, Uncle Sal looked like he could go for some drugs about now, and Pam was looking as pissed as ever.

On my part, I found myself awkwardly glancing around the gym and appraising my future classmates.

That was when I saw her. This sadly numb, hurt, broken girl. Pretty, but not in an obvious or overblown manner. Looking strangely forlorn in a tough-guy, I'll-keep-it-all-inside way.

Sydney.

I can't explain what drew me to her, what made the entire world stop the moment I saw her. I only know that it did.

Let me pause here for a moment to interject some important material about my love life.

I don't know any way to say this without sounding dreadfully arrogant, so I'll just put it bluntly: I am a rather good-looking chap. It's not a bit of my own doing, so I've really no right to be high and mighty about it, but it's the truth, nonetheless. So that means that, growing up (think, even back before puberty made me quite understand what was going on), girls rather tended to flock to me. Again, I know it sounds terribly pompous, but such was my cross. I'm being quite serious when I say this. Because of course in the beginning around age thirteen or fourteen, all was jolly good and my poor mum barely knew what to do with me, as I stepped out with girl after girl who was over the moon for me. But then things got difficult. It seems that most teenagers of the general sort, once they reach a certain age, have expectations of the type of behavior they'll be engaging in with a date. That is to say, my "good Catholic boy" persona complicated matters. Because, after all, I was a good Catholic boy in reality and not just persona, and well, none of these girls after me were exactly good Catholic girls. In short, my good looks made girls assume I was sexually experienced. Which I was not in the least, nor wished to be pre-wedding night.

And so, through no real choice of my own but more out of necessity, my dating life came to a crashing halt by about age sixteen and a half. Mostly, I was okay with that. No need to rush things. I always assumed that eventually, God willing, I'd find a girl on the same page as me about these things and fall in love. You know, the gradual way that most people fall in love, some time after getting to know the other person.

Not at first sight.

I denied it.

So there was a girl across the way . . . So what? So bloody what? I didn't know her name or a singular thing about her, so there was no reason on earth that I should give in to the longing to look her way again. And no reason that I should suddenly picture myself at the altar, her in a white gown beside me. Get a grip, old boy, you're at a bloody funeral!

I exhaled. Stared at my shoes. Get a grip, indeed. Must

be exhaustion, physical and emotional. For surely this was neither the time nor the place to pick up chicks, as they say.

Valiantly, I ignored all this, determined to deny that my world had just changed radically. And I turned my attention back to this alleged new family.

Pam was bouncing her leg in agitation. Oh goody, here's an attention-suck for me. Because clearly something was really wrong with her just then. It was actually so obvious and distracting that I was legitimately able to focus on it and pretend that I could forget about the girl I'd just seen.

I leaned in close to Pam to whisper an inquiry of whether she was okay, but she shot me a glance that said more clearly than words, "Don't you dare even think about opening your bloody mouth."

Well then.

I sat back. But continued to observe her covertly.

It was during the eulogy that Pam finally reached a boiling point. After minutes on end of the leg-bouncing, crossed arms, sighing, and terribly pissed-off face, she finally could take it no longer.

A group of Josh's former teammates were together at the lectern in support as one of them struggled through some words about what a great guy their pal was. "He was so much fun to—to be around. And he inspired us, constantly . . . to be better."

And Pam was all but shaking, rocking back and forth, looking ready to punch someone in the face. I was now staring at her unabashedly, really only wondering how her parents weren't noticing, let alone the rest of the gym.

Pam finally whispered, "Screw this shit," and sprang up to leave.

Aunt Jem paused her weeping to look at her daughter, startled, but Pam couldn't have cared less and just shoved her way out.

I stood immediately to follow, whispering, "I've got this," to Aunt Jem.

I followed Pam out of the gym to the hallway, where she immediately punched a locker door, apparently unaware that I was behind her. She shook her hand in pain, swearing some more over it, when I startled her by saying, "Is that as therapeutic as it looks?"

She whirled to face me. "Leave me alone."

I calmly stood my ground. "Well, I do like to fix things. And I probably can't do much to fix any of this, I understand, but that won't stop me from trying."

We stood there a moment, her staring at me, deciding. Finally: "You wanna know? You want the burden of knowledge?"

"If I can help you carry it."

She didn't spill it immediately. She crossed her arms, exhaled, bounced her leg. "Fine. My brother was an asshole."

This didn't shock me as much as I might have wished. "Okay."

"Not a regular asshole. Like he was that too, and if that was all, it'd be like whatever. But it's not all. He was one hundred percent douchebag terrible."

"Pam, what? What did he do?"

She turned and stared me straight in the eye. "He *raped* some girl. Like hours before he died. And then, as he's freaking lying there in the hospital, when he made me come in close to whisper something? He tells me about it. And he has the balls to say he hopes he doesn't go to hell!"

I was speechless, truly floored, as I finally discovered the depths of this tragedy.

And now, at long last, she couldn't take it anymore. Her angry tears were flying everywhere. Instinct took over, and before either of us knew what had happened I was holding her as she sobbed against me.

—

Sydney made it through the rest of the funeral somehow on autopilot, amazed at her own ability to turn off emotion and sit through prayers for Josh's soul that a large part of her didn't want to participate in, and praises for his character that would have made her vomit if she truly thought about what was being said.

As it all ended, she found herself sticking to her parents' side, because she knew now that the hopefully imaginary stares were in fact quite real. Only, the parental shield wasn't really working as she might have hoped. Many of her classmates continued making moves to come offer her comfort, commiseration. She barely managed polite facial acknowledgment and mostly let Winnie take over, conscious all the while that a relieving picture of what her social life might actually look like was forming in her mother's head.

But then this trendy hipster fellow in his mid-twenties sought Sydney out. She could see him in her peripherals and had a feeling he was coming for her as she stood with Winnie and her parents in the long line leading to the wake in the student center next door; so she quickly repositioned herself on the other side of her parents and kept her head down. Not knowing exactly why, she was positive that she wanted nothing to do with this guy right now.

He wasn't fazed. "Sydney? Excuse me, you're Sydney Camden, right?" He just kind of weaseled his way in there.

She tried to ignore him, but he got even closer before Winnie said abruptly, "Who the hell are you?"

Robert gave the man a discreet stare that rather matched Winnie's words, if one was looking, while Maryanne snipped, "Excuse us. Our daughter's a little upset right now."

The guy said, "Oh of course. My condolences. My name is Andy Carlson. I'm with the *Star*. I was just hoping I'd be able to get a quote from . . . Josh's girlfriend?"

Sydney felt as if the air had left her lungs, hearing these words out loud. Knowing the entire school assumed she was grieving him deeply wasn't quite the same caliber of hideousness as having a complete stranger call her Josh's girlfriend.

She looked away, tried to compose herself, pretend this wasn't happening. She was pretending a lot these days. Sometimes, it worked. This was not one of those times.

The guy pressed. "You must be devastated, I can only imagine. Would you be willing to give me a brief quote? On how you're feeling, what he meant to you—"

Winnie said, "Listen, asshat—"

And Robert, coming more fully out of his own land of nuclear physics and assessing that his cold stare wasn't getting the job done, cut in. "We'd appreciate some privacy right now, thank you."

"Oh, sure." And before this Andy Carlson could leave like a decent person, Sydney's Aunt Lisa swooped in.

"Andy, what the hell are you doing? Don't be a vulture! Can't you see she wants to be left alone?"

Sydney was practically dying with relief as her beautiful, levelheaded aunt wrapped her arm around Sydney and shooed the guy away. "Sorry, hon. Some people, right? That guy, Andy, he's a total baby writer. He graduated like the day before yesterday." Sydney cracked a small smile. "You think I'm kidding. No seriously, he's been with us over a month and hasn't cracked a story yet. A little desperate these days. Next thing you know he'll be chasing *ambulances*!" This last sentence was said loudly in the guy's direction, a parting shot as Lisa steered her grateful niece farther away.

And then Lisa was giving Sydney's mother a quick hug of greeting, and a stiff-awkward side-hug to Robert, leaving Sydney with a moment to compose herself. Winnie was glancing at her anxiously, aware that Sydney had seemed, on the whole, to be near some kind of nervous breakdown throughout the entire event. But right now, Sydney was just letting herself revel in her dear aunt's non-smothering comfort and letting herself look the misery she felt, blocking firmly and purposefully from her mind the actual reasons for that misery.

8

AS MUCH AS SYDNEY had been able to internally deny and outwardly pretend in the matter of her misery, the next morning found her facing the real problem anew, more clearly than ever.

The Saturday morning paper stared at her with its mocking headline: SPRING BREAK TRAGEDY, above a large picture of Josh in his football uniform. The byline confirmed that the story was written by that weasel-vulture Andy Carlson.

She picked the paper up, because she had to know. Scanned, hoping to not see . . . And there it was: "Sydney Camden, Simpson's girlfriend . . ." And even a tidbit more about her being the rising star playwright prodigy of St. Aloysius Academy, just in case anyone reading it might have missed the reference to her name alone.

She felt bile rise up her throat as her stomach churned. She dropped the paper to the counter and dashed to the sink, and she emptied the contents of her stomach.

Maryanne came trotting from her home office around the corner at the sound. Sydney quickly wiped her mouth and tried to pretend she hadn't just horror-puked. "Honey? Are you okay? Did you throw up?"

"I'm fine. I was . . . kind of gagging? I think I . . . must have been choking?" More half-truths. The thought did nothing to settle her churning stomach.

Maryanne patted her on the back. "You're sure you're okay now?" Sydney nodded in response, and Maryanne seemed satisfied. Until she noticed the huge story in the paper sitting there beside Sydney. "How are you otherwise, sweetie? With all this?" Referencing the dreadful paper, of course.

Sydney gulped. Her own mother was thinking the same as the rest of the world about her and Josh. Sydney's own fault. Theoretically, she could set her mother straight about it all. Right here, right now. But the thought sent a fresh rush of terrible adrenaline over Sydney and she felt she just couldn't. So instead she said, "I'm fine," and slipped off up the stairs.

Once in the sanctuary of her room, Sydney started pacing, her mind racing in a million directions that she didn't want to explore. She *couldn't* be seen as Josh's girlfriend, not after what he did to her, how she essentially hated him, irrationally feared him (irrational, of course, because of his deadness), wallowed in the utter brokenness caused by him. Even before he took things too far, she'd known she wasn't crazy about him and had been trying to admit to herself that she really didn't want him as her boyfriend. But to be seen as his girlfriend *now*? She felt her breath coming faster, as if the walls were closing in. She had to change this. Some way. Somehow.

Forcing herself to calm down, she sat at her desk. And she went for her ever-trusty notebook, fingers itching.

How to proceed? Write a scene in which she was brave enough to admit to the world what he'd done to her? The thought made her want to puke again. Even to do so in semi-fiction was unbearable. Write something in which everyone forgot about her and any association she'd ever had with Josh? More possible, but still not quite right. What had happened was still sitting on her chest, its weight a constant reminder, and she didn't think imagining that people had forgotten about her would change that. Especially when, in a couple of days at school, she would be faced anew with their attention.

There was one other possibility for comfort-writing that came to her. It was almost too gruesome to consider. But she thought that, just maybe, she might be able to lose herself temporarily in thoughts of a more pleasant alternate reality than what had *really* happened. Heck, she had already almost seemed to have changed real-life events with what she wrote of Josh dying that night. Why not give it a try again? It defied good sense, thinking like this. But she was desperate.

Almost recklessly, she dove in. *I, Sydney Camden, was Josh's girlfriend. We loved each other very much.*

She began writing a scene of the two of them on a date. Only, but for his outward appearance, this fellow was not Josh at all. Rather, he was a perfect gentleman, charming and attentive, asking her the perfect questions and sharing little jokes with her. They were in a restaurant, and he was pulling out the chair for her, then seating himself across from her and locking his loving, adoring gaze on her. It was perfection. Until…

Tragic death, gone too early, leaving loved ones behind. A tragedy worthy of Shakespeare.

And then, *After the accident,* she wrote, *I missed him deeply.*

Thank goodness I had so many loving friends to get me through it. And she wrote a scene in her living room. She was surrounded by Winnie and some of those girls who offered her condolences at the funeral. They comforted her as she cried. *Even my parents knew just what I needed.* And now Maryanne was coming around the corner, holding a smiley, gurgling toddler. *"I know how much you've always hated being an only child, Sydney. So we went ahead and adopted a little sister! I won't be smothering you anymore!"* This made Sydney smile, and she wiped her tears to stand up and go google at the baby. Only to be interrupted by Robert's sudden appearance. His arms were wide open. *"Sydney, do you need a hug from Daddy? I'm sorry I've always been so cold and distant."* And she dived into his arms. A perfect picture, the two of them with Maryanne snuggling the baby nearby. *So even though it was painful, I gradually began to heal from the loss of my boyfriend, Josh.*

There, it was finished. It was hideous, much more clichéd and stilted than her normal caliber of story, but it was everything she thought she wanted to feel right now.

A little harrowed but triumphant, she dropped her pen to the desk. She felt victorious. She had written it. So maybe she could live it, externally. Pretend. And not throw up about it anymore.

She hopped up to pace again, psyching herself up. She had done it. She was strong. She could cope. She could change all this.

But could she? Really and truly? She wanted to, but she had to test it, come to know what she could handle. And preferably before school started again.

She grabbed her phone and dialed Winnie. Because she knew Winnie was planning to go to a party tonight.

Despite being the day after the funeral of the school's golden boy, it was apparently time for one last spring break celebration. It was probably in honor of Josh for all she knew. But Sydney told herself that she didn't care one bit about the why or how. Rather, her only concern with this party was to test herself and her ability to carry this secret around for the rest of her life, even among her classmates who now believed something very different from the reality she had experienced.

So, though she never had before in her life, tonight she was going to party.

———

As for me that night, I was minding my own business sitting on my cot, which was still surrounded by Josh's mounds of crap since no one had had the heart to go through anything yet. I was reading one of the few books I'd come across in the entire house—some inane modern American novel that was shaping up to be about as spectacular as my general existence here—when Pam knocked on the half-open door.

"Calvin?"

I dropped the book. It was no match for interaction with an actual person. "Yes?

"There's a party tonight. I think it's ridiculous, but they say they're doing it for Josh."

I waited. She didn't go on. "Did you want to go?"

"No!" A pause. "I mean, I *don't*, but the word is that *she's* gonna be there."

"The girl?" I should mention that this conversation between us took place minutes after Sydney made the call to tell Winnie she wanted to go. Apparently, word travels fast among the students of St. Aloysius, and former school joke

Sydney Camden planning to attend the party was obviously rather newsworthy.

Pam nodded. "The girl he raped. And I don't know . . . maybe she's gonna talk? About what he did? Trash him to everyone?"

I motioned her to take a seat beside me on the cot. She wrinkled her nose at the refuse between her and it, shaking her head. "Is she the type to do that, do you think?" I asked, thinking it a relevant question but of course feeling no pressing personal curiosity about the nature of this victim who was still anonymous to me. Pam shrugged in response, crossing her arms. I asked, "She never went to the coppers about it, right?"

"As far as I know, you and I are the only other ones in the world who know what he did."

It sounded so weighty to hear her say it like that. "So what makes you think it might happen tonight?"

"Well, she's not really a chick who goes to parties. The fact that she's supposedly gonna be there is kind of weird in itself. I have to wonder if, like now that the funeral is over with, she wants to get her revenge by telling everyone." Pam finally braved the mounds of crap, stepping over them as best as she could to take a seat beside me. And she let out a big, frustrated sigh. "Which is why I have to go. No one's gonna believe her."

I felt like I was missing a piece of the puzzle (and had no idea that I was in fact missing several). "Why not?

"She's not exactly well-liked . . ."

It didn't take me long to understand what I needed to do for my poor cousin here. I stood up and pulled her to her feet. "When should we leave?"

Sydney arrived at this party with Winnie and immediately discovered that everything she had stereotypically expected of a high school party but had never actually seen was absolutely true: loud music, dancing, making out, and plenty of booze.

Winnie watched her as they stepped inside. Because Sydney, despite her resolutions, didn't quite look like someone ready to party. Rather, she was taking big, calming breaths, trying with all her might to emit confidence.

"You sure you've got this?" Winnie asked.

Sydney barely had a chance to nod in reply before some girl who had never given her the time of day before spotted her.

"Sydney! I'm so glad you made it! Josh totally would have wanted it this way. It's great you're here." And the girl started leading her into the middle of it all, forcing Sydney to up her *I'm-being-strong* face.

Winnie watched her being led away, satisfied that she seemed to be handling it, and took to amusing herself.

And this is precisely when we arrived.

I knew immediately that this was not my scene. I glanced at Pam beside me and knew she didn't want to be here either. She was scanning the room, intent, so I fought the urge to ask if she was sure she wanted to do this. Instead, I just clapped a hand on her shoulder in support, which she pretended to ignore.

And then she apparently spotted the girl. "I think I have to do this alone," she said. I nodded and moved to a spot against the wall as I watched her disappear into the crowd.

I had only been standing there a moment, hardly even long enough to decide whether or not I was feeling awkward about it, when a girl came along. A flirty, made-up, wannabe model–type of girl. Which, incidentally, had never been my type of girl.

"You don't go to St. Al, do you?" Kendall asked me, by way of introduction.

"Oh, um, I've been told I do, starting Monday."

She gasped, delighted. "You're British!" Nothing gets past you.

Out of my sight line and earshot, Pam was across the room, nearing a group of girls who were gathered around Sydney. Pam was glad to see that Sydney looked strong, emboldened, capable. Surely Sydney was really going to do it, then. Pam steeled herself to hear it, to confirm it and to help Sydney let the world know what a terrible person her brother had been.

And instead, Pam arrived on the edge of the circle just in time to hear Sydney say, "I'm trying to hold on to the memories I have with him . . ."

One of the other girls put a comforting hand on Sydney's arm. "You're so strong, Sydney."

Pam couldn't believe her ears, and she couldn't help herself. "What!"

And now Sydney wheeled around. Saw Pam. Though the two of them had never spoken in person, Sydney knew who she was.

Sydney's entire demeanor changed instantly. The resilience, the strength, her show of confidence, all withered and died quite suddenly. She seemed to shrivel, to wilt, as she stared at Pam and Pam stared back at her. Mutual horror.

Pam gathered her voice. "What is *wrong* with you? After…" But Pam was starting to understand a little, realizing that Sydney was pretending for some reason, as she took in the frantic pleading in Sydney's eyes and the staring faces of the other girls. Pam shook her head. Giving up. "Gone bat-shit crazy but doing just fine."

And as Pam turned to shove her way back out through the crowd, the other girls turned to Sydney with questions. "What was that about?" And, "What's wrong with *her*? You're just mourning like a normal person."

Sydney did her best to agree facially, but she had to get away. This was too much to keep up right now.

She was pushing her way out through the crowd, much more successfully than Pam was. And suddenly, I saw Sydney. I recognized her immediately as the girl I'd seen at the funeral and had pretended to forget about ever since.

This girl Kendall was still trying her best to violently flirt with me, and I was oblivious to it as I followed Sydney with my gaze.

I wasn't at a funeral anymore, and this girl looked more distressed than ever. Having no idea that Pam was already on the way back and would be hoping to find me for a quick exit, I abruptly excused myself from Kendall and moved to follow Sydney outside.

I don't know what I was expecting, or what I was hoping, considering that I had firmly told myself there was absolutely no reason in the world to fancy myself in love with this girl I'd never so much as spoken to. But I couldn't deny that following her felt like the thing to do.

I stepped out onto the porch and stopped in my tracks, for the girl was near hyperventilation, pacing and muttering to herself. I couldn't really understand her, but in actuality she was saying, "We loved each other very much … perfect gentleman … miss him deeply …" Trying her damnedest to make everything okay in her mind, when Pam's confrontation had zapped her quite thoroughly into remembrance that nothing was okay at all.

I watched her a moment, aware that she didn't seem to know I was there behind her, and yet thinking I couldn't possibly startle her much. I tried clearing my throat, but she missed it over the noise of additional cars pulling in behind us. So I stepped a little closer. I reached out, and I gently put a hand on her shoulder to get her attention.

She jumped, practically into the air. And turned to stare at me. I stared back. There was a brief, confused terror in her eyes, and she backed away from me.

"What's wrong?" I asked, advancing innocently, still oblivious to the fact that I had stumbled upon the very girl Pam had come here for, a girl who had every reason to act so strangely. But she just continued backing away, looking more and more like a caged animal. And she started to close her eyes, in a way only someone deadly embarrassed would do. Which meant she didn't realize how close she was to the porch railing behind her.

Several things happened at once. She let out a yelp, I abruptly shot out a hand to try to steady her, she tried to rip herself father back from my reach, and she fell quite over the railing. I had a strange feeling of being watched but ignored it as she hopped up and took off running like she could outrun her mortification.

I nearly hopped over the railing myself after her, more in hopes of finding answers than anything else. But before I could even grab on firmly to swing over, I heard a, "Freeze!"

I turned and realized suddenly that the additional cars pulling in had in fact been cops coming to bust up the party, because behind me was none other than my pal Frownie Cop.

Though I obediently froze, I couldn't help but quip, "You again? I must be the new highlight of your beat." But he was clearly in no joking mood. He had cuffs ready for me. Behind him, his comrades were already bursting inside to bust up the party. "Erm," I stalled, "I can assure you this wasn't at all what it looked like." While I wondered what exactly it *had* looked like. Quite possibly like I was a would-be attacker, considering the handcuff business about to go down. No good. My mind raced. This was all circumstantial, obviously, as I wasn't even one of the drunk partiers. Certainly nothing I could actually be charged with for talking to a nervous girl.

But the cuffs were snapping on, nonetheless, as he said, "Of course it wasn't."

"Listen," I said, trying not to sound as desperate as I felt while he started pushing me toward his patrol car. "What you just saw here was a total misunderstanding. Not sure I even understood it myself. And I definitely haven't been drinking. I showed up here not ten minutes ago and haven't touched a drop. See, smell my breath."

And yes, I breathed in his face. He cringed. "Ugh, salami and ... cream soda?"

I was tempted to throw in a joke about alcoholic

consumption being legal for a guy my age in my home country, but I thought better of it and only said, "Unless my halitosis is a crime, I should think a warning would be appropriate here. Haven't you got better things to be doing in there?"

I could tell it was killing Frownie Cop, but he glanced over his shoulder at all the commotion of wild teens running off, climbing out windows and whatnot, and it was obvious he should be helping attend to them. He reluctantly took my cuffs off. "Consider this strike two."

I backed away, rubbing my wrists, and blimey I just couldn't resist: "Yes, of course. I'll work on keeping that strike rate up. Love the cricket analogy, very culturally sensitive of you!"

And I trotted out away toward the street, glancing anxiously this way and that for a sight of Pam.

Luckily, she was hurrying out with the other escapees from the side. She spotted me, and we raced to meet at the side of the road where we'd left our bikes. Without a word, we both hopped on and started peddling away like mad.

I let a few moments go by before probing. "So the girl. She was there?" Pam nodded, rather sullen. "And did she do it, then? Come out about it?" Her scowl only settled in further. "What happened?"

"She's freaking marvelous. Pretending to mourn him like the dying part is all there is to it. That chick is *screwed up*. But she clearly doesn't need me."

"... She might."

"No way. She can keep her head up her ass, but I'm sure as hell not going in there."

I didn't know it at the time, but Pam's crude assessment of the situation was all too true.

SYDNEY WAS INDEED, as Pam had put it, rather screwed up, living in her world of purposeful denial. Sydney really did know full well what she was doing, suspected it might not be healthy, but couldn't think of a better alternative and so spiraled deeper into denial.

She could hardly think even a little of what had just gone down on that porch without wishing to hide herself in some deep dark hole. Even in the best of circumstances, being caught muttering to oneself when everyone else is inside enjoying a party would be rather embarrassing. But Sydney's incident was wrapped up with this elaborate deception she was trying to enforce upon herself, and with the knowledge that at least Pam knew it wasn't true.

Sydney wanted to change it all.

Even as she ran off from the encounter with me, she was already doing her best to forget what had just happened. She kept running, the whole one-point-two miles home, focusing on the movements of her body and on emptying her mind of the unpleasant interactions she'd just experienced.

By the time she neared home, she had slowed to a trot and was able to calm herself to a level at which she suspected she might look like nothing was amiss. Giving herself one last quick going-over of straightening, she went inside.

She had told her parents yet another half-truth about hanging out with Winnie for the evening, so even her mother barely gave her a second glance or thought as they headed up to bed. Sydney rather marveled at this, glancing in the mirror and amazed to see that she did indeed look perfectly normal. Nothing wrong, and nothing out of the ordinary going on in her life. It heartened her, in this desperate quest of hers to pretend and forget.

So she went up to her own room and dialed Winnie, assuming that Winnie would be worried sick at her disappearance, and rather worried herself that Winnie had landed in jail for underage drinking.

But instead, she found that not only was Winnie aggravatingly unworried about Sydney's fate for the evening, the girl was actually out doing some celebratory drinking with a few other lucky escapees. Sydney hung up quickly, more conscious than ever of how their paths seemed to be diverging lately.

She stared at her desk a moment before deciding instinctively that inaction would begin to drive her to despair. So she grabbed her notebook once again.

This time, she changed the party. There wasn't so very much wrong with it, only the part where Pam and that annoying handsome stranger (me) showed up, jolting her toward harsh reality. So she simply left that part out, keeping the elements of what she thought her new normalcy should be—the other girls comforting her and accepting her, the feeling of oneness with them as they mourned Josh and celebrated his life. It kind of made her sick, but she ignored that sentiment and powered on.

All would be well, she was mildly sure of it, if only she could pretend that this was the way things really were.

As for me, I was doing some pretending of my own.

Pam and I went home, to a predictably sterile and lonely home. She didn't seem inclined to any further conversation or socializing, so I let her go her own way and tried to amuse myself with various reading and online social media perusal. But looking at other people's cat videos was not doing the trick to keep my mind off the evening's bizarre and disturbing experiences, so I decided to venture out of that swamp hole that was my room.

It *was* rather late, but Pam's light was still on. So I knocked. "What!" was her surly response.

I cleared my throat. "It's me. Calvin." No response. "Can I come in?"

"As long as it's not to talk about the party."

Hmm. There goes that. I went in anyway.

Her room was rather less destroyed than her late brother's, but it was still full of a random assortment of décor that did little to shed light on any singular traits of her personality: strange assortment of musical group posters, spanning the range of grunge metal to country; girly items like a jewelry box and stuffed animals, partially hidden out of sight; and a surprising amount of books, of the classic literature variety.

I pounced on the books as the most promising line of conversation. "An Austen fan? I wouldn't have guessed."

"Why not?" she asked, a little defensive.

I merely shrugged. "Not a lot of people our age have the patience." That seemed to satisfy her, but she went back to her task—painting her toenails a dark blue that was almost a clichéd black but not quite. She did, however, have only one ear bud in, the empty ear about as near an invitation as she was probably going to give me.

I sat down at her desk. "Want to *not* think about the party together?"

"Not really."

"Well then here's something totally unrelated to think about: Has your mom ever happened to have mentioned anything about my mom and the time she got pregnant with me? Like maybe who in the bloody goodness my father might be?"

That got her attention. But she shook her head. "She's a pretty closed book about her childhood and growing up and crap."

"Hmm. Any old diaries or anything we could raid?"

She scoffed. "Can you picture my uptight mother as some giggling teenage girl with a diary?"

"I don't know that it would require giggling . . ."

Her wheels were turning though. "We could try the photo albums in the attic if you were really desperate."

"Boom. Let's do it."

Then followed a couple hours of jokes and laughter at terrible British '90s clothes as the two of us pored over stacks of old photos in the attic. We had to first dig through some old pictures of Pam and Josh as kids, many of which contained hints that he was not exactly a smashing big brother: Josh hoarding toys or smacking her, Pam crying to the side in some of these pre-digital camera shots. She didn't comment on it, but I began to think her life might have been far from rosy even before now. And I began to resolve to be the best replacement big brother I could be—until momentarily, that felt weird, as if I was trying to weasel in where I didn't belong, taking a dead guy's place. So I shook off the thoughts altogether and returned to the task at hand. And we laughed and we joked, and it felt like the perfect antidote to the terribleness of life for both of us lately.

Bonding with her had been at least a secondary goal for this late-night adventure, the primary one being to actually find information on my alleged father. And I was about to give up on the primary with a "secondary mission accomplished," when she exclaimed, "Here they are with guys!"

I looked at the picture eagerly. We'd seen nothing like it yet, so it was at least a bit promising. I carefully pulled the picture out of its sleeve for a closer look.

Teenaged Jem and my mum were dressed for some sort of formal dance. Jem was looking none too thrilled with her date, but my mum was looking absolutely enamored with the handsome fellow who had his arm around her. A handsome fellow who looked frighteningly like me.

"That's him," I pronounced.

Pam peered at it critically. "Totally has to be." She took the picture from my hand and turned it over. There was writing on the back. *2000 Winter Formal, Jem and Jan with dates Carl Peterson and Thomas Tucker.* "And there you go. Name."

"Damn," I said softly. "Couldn't have been something un-pronounceable and easy to locate? How many Thomas Tuckers must there be in this country?"

She shrugged. "It's a good start, probably."

I nodded. It probably was. And more importantly, it was something substantial to latch onto in my mind, something hopeful, and something that had absolutely nothing to do with the nutso girl I feared I loved.

Pam turned to me. "I hope you can find him. I hope something good can happen to someone in this house."

"Thank you," I said, all the while thinking that it already had. For, at least to me, the two of us felt so much closer and like maybe we had found a friend in each other. I so didn't want to ruin it, but I felt there were worlds of things she must need to talk about and discuss, concerning Josh and faith and life in general. So I dared and ventured to ask, "Do you want to talk about Josh yet?"

Her facial expression immediately closed. I thought for a moment that she might yell, cuss me out, maybe even hit me. But then, as if she could actually sense my sincerity and desire to help, she shook her head softly. "Not yet." She handed the picture back to me. "Might as well keep it. No one will miss it." And she stood to go to bed.

I watched her leave, my heart feeling torn and pulled in several different weighty directions.

Perhaps all in good time. Just now, it was time for sleep and a restful Sunday before beginning what I suspected was to be a momentous school change for me.

———

Sydney was not privileged with a restful Sunday at all, because she also suspected that her return to school would be momentous, but in a very different way than my own momentousness. For her, rather than a new beginning, it was to be a test of whether her old trials were actually gone, and of whether she could truly keep up the pretense that might bring such a thing about. So obviously, she could hardly sleep the night before, let alone relax while awake.

Monday morning dawned, and Sydney tried to steel her nerves, tell herself that her own confidence was the key to all this. That this was her chance at the happy ending she had always wanted. But she didn't believe herself, because beneath the shallow veil of pretense were memories and pieces of knowledge that were anything but happy. And she didn't know if she could keep it up.

So, first thing in the morning, she went back to what she had written, added to it even, dove deep into the story. Ignored the cautionary part that reminded her how trippy such an exercise had seemed back when she'd first tried it at age twelve. Because now, if her reality and fiction started to blend, she certainly couldn't be any worse off, she reasoned, considering that the fiction was so far superior to her present reality.

As she walked through the doors to her place of torture once again that morning, she was on pins and needles to see if her recent treatment and status would last. Maybe she would go back to being a nobody, which would be fine. Or the butt of frequent jokes, which would be less fine. But Winnie beside her was saying, "I'm telling you, your old spot on the food chain is gone."

If the words didn't exactly give Sydney confidence, they perhaps at least gave her the small shove she needed to emit a look that was near confidence. And she quipped back, "Well where'd it go?"

"To some lowly freshman?

"Maybe a poor asthmatic band geek?"

Winnie nodded agreement, relaxing at what sounded suspiciously like the old Sydney back in full force. And

Sydney could feel it too, that she seemed normal and fine, so she tried to roll with that feeling and believe it.

Which got easier when a slalom of female well-wishers began greeting her. "Sydney, how you holding up?" "You look great, girl." "Hang in there. It'll get easier, I promise."

Sydney took it all with a graceful smile, sharing incredulous glances with the smug Winnie. But then they neared Kendall lounging against her locker. Winnie whispered, "You're grieving. She can't touch you without looking like a bitch." So Sydney tried her best and managed to actually walk semi-confidently past, without sparing a glance for her torturer.

And then, just when Sydney started to get cocky and think that maybe she could have a true handle on this new dynamic, she realized a guy was headed her way. She recognized him. It was one of Josh's jock friends, a guy who had probably said mocking things about her dozens of times. Likely, he was about to offer her condolences, as everyone else seemed to be doing. Surely it was just more of the same. But it felt different. She wasn't sure why, but she wanted to turn and run away. In the seconds it took him to advance, her mind sped, trying to understand why she was afraid. Was the possibility of more insults really a big deal at this point? Possibly. But irrationally, what she suspected she really feared was that this fellow would be lusting after her as Josh had. Irrational, because surely even if he did he wouldn't act on it here and now. She knew this, and she tried to talk down her speeding heart rate with such logic. A failure.

She whispered to Winnie, "Interference?"

With a sigh, Winnie smoothly drifted in behind Sydney, to her other side, so that she was between Sydney and the guy.

"Sydney, how are you holding up?" the guy said.

And Sydney managed a polite look of acknowledgment while Winnie took over. "She's hanging in there." Then Winnie dropped her voice and said to Sydney, "He's just a guy, ya know. A few weeks ago he wouldn't have given you the time of day."

"Except to make fun of me."

"Exactly."

Sydney sighed, shook her head, not wanting to admit how afraid she felt. "Just keep this up a little longer?"

And this precise moment is when she passed me in the hall. Instinctively, I looked up. And we met eyes.

She froze. I froze. But both of us for different reasons.

Her, because the sight of me brought back her awkward and unpleasant memories from the party, knowing she must have looked like an absolute crazy person to me.

Me, because I was once again blown away by the sight of her.

This frozen phenomenon lasted only a moment, until she quickened her pace and thoroughly ignored me. At least outwardly. As I would later learn, she was actually wrestling with a blip of attraction toward me, trying not to think about how the two of us maybe could have met in some fantastically romantic fashion and have been on our way to a great love story, if only she hadn't first laid eyes on me in the middle of a terrible personal crisis. And thinking like this was comforting. Our terrible meeting meant that she *couldn't* harbor romantic feelings toward me, which meant she sure didn't have to worry about anything turning out like the last fellow she'd liked.

I couldn't help but stare after her, transfixed despite

myself and despite the indications that this girl was to be off limits for me. And of course all I saw was the back of her head, and Winnie gawking at me.

Just now, Winnie was actually saying to Sydney about me, "Okay I will be *all* about running interference with that guy. Hell, I'll get physical if I need to."

To which Sydney responded unconvincingly, "What guy."

—

After our brief hallway meeting, I wasn't really expecting much more eventfulness that morning, just more of the same curious looks unaccompanied by any form of inquiry or introduction, as I had been getting since I walked through the doors with Pam. And I certainly didn't expect to be so fortunate as to begin my next encounter with Sydney but a few minutes later.

Imagine my delight when I entered the classroom for what was to be my first period American literature class and saw her sitting there in the front row. However, despite my being in her direct line of sight, she refused to see me. So I slipped into a seat near the back and forced my eyes to leave the object of my attention. Clearly she had no interest in me, despite the supposed draw of my dashing looks, so I would probably be best to focus on getting myself a good education in what these Americans called literature for the next two months.

The start bell rang, and the teacher, an idealistic but undeniably tired bloke by the name of Mr. Sanders, jumped right in. "I expect you've all finished the reading by now. Any volunteers to summarize and explain the use of symbolism, starting with Hester's daughter, Pearl?"

Sydney immediately raised her hand. As for every other student in the classroom, they avoided eye contact. "Anyone other than Sydney today?" He stared down a few students before finally landing on one particularly unfortunate girl.

"How is Pearl a symbol?" she asked. "Isn't she a character?"

Mr. Sanders only sighed. "Take it away, Sydney."

Sydney was more than ready. "Pearl *is* a character, but her primary function through most of the book is as a symbol, a physical consequence of Hester's transgression. Pearl is a living representation of Hester's punishment, but she's also a blessing to Hester…"

Okay. Forget Hawthorne. Sydney was the real story here. I couldn't help it. I was becoming more and more intrigued with each passing moment.

But I also couldn't quite miss what was going on beside me. There was a guy blatantly rolling his eyes at Sydney, only to be cuffed by the girl next to him. The guy turned to that girl, his face asking, **What the hell?** And the girl responded with a look that clearly said, **Shame on you!**

Of course I understood none of this yet, having no clue of Sydney's involvement with Josh in any fashion or of her former social status. So I disregarded what I'd just seen and turned my attention back to Sydney as she finished. "The paradox is that while Pearl is living proof of Hester's sin, she's also the only thing that makes Hester's resulting social exile bearable."

If I had known Sydney and had been accustomed to her look in normal circumstances, I might have noticed that, smoothly as she had seemed to deliver all this, she did falter a little here and there, with a slight blush as she vaguely referenced the sexual aspects of the story. Because even though she knew the story inside and out, had analyzed it coldly and thoroughly, a tale revolving around a troublesome sexual act was hitting a bit too close to home for her right now. She tried to ignore thoughts of any connection to her own circumstances, and the academic setting mostly won out for her attention. And of course, considering the drama going down all around her, no one noticed her minuscule faltering.

Mr. Sanders didn't seem to notice it either—after all, her delivery was still about three thousand percent more polished than even the best of his other students. So he responded, "Very good, Sydney." And then to the rest of the class, "Anything to add? Comments? Nothing?" He was looking at them expectantly, in a bad way, a way that said, *Let's get this over with.* And everyone was shifting awkwardly, again avoiding eye contact. "Well, very good. Perhaps you've all finally decided to grow up and appreciate what an asset Sydney is to this class. Sydney, I assume you've already completed the paper?" She had it in her hands. Mr. Sanders took it. "Marvelous. I'll be posting her paper as an example again, and like always you'd do well to utilize it."

Rather in awe, I gazed at her. Who was this girl? The back of her head gave me nothing in way of answer.

10

IT'S QUITE POSSIBLE that by this point in our story, I should have taken the huge cosmic hint that this girl was not exactly a prime candidate for me to pursue.

And yet, come lunch period of that first day, I was faced with a choice. I stared at the cafeteria full of strangers before me, any one of whom could have become my new best mate, even several girls who had the potential to be all I ever wanted in a girlfriend/eventual wife. If I had wanted to, I could have put on my outgoing pants and introduced myself. I probably could have had my pick of anyone in the whole place to eat my lunch with.

But I didn't do that. Why would I want to? Cosmic hints and all, Sydney was a much more appealing choice, though I didn't know fully why.

So she didn't seem to want to acknowledge my existence. So what? Surely we could get around that hurdle. I brought my tray over to the table where she sat with Winnie.

Sydney saw me and looked anywhere else. I continued on, undeterred. "Hello there!" I greeted them. "Mind if I sit?"

Winnie's eyes lit up. "And he's got an accent! Please do!"

I was aware that Sydney was still not looking at me, rather squirmy, uncomfortable. And I was determined to wait out whatever was making her respond so to me, until she could be won over by my undeniable charm.

I held out a hand. "I'm Calvin."

And Winnie pounced on it. "I'm Winnie." I looked to Sydney, waiting for her to act similarly. She didn't. She merely stared down at her food, looking like the personification of the fight-or-flight instinct.

Silence. Uncomfortable silence. Winnie tried to fill it with some awkward giggle-like thing, but even she was glancing uncomfortably at her friend.

Finally, I tried to joke, "Did I do something to her?"

That was apparently much too complicated a question for Winnie to answer. "Um..."

Never mind. "You know what? I'm a sensitive guy. I can take a hint." I picked up my tray to leave, conscious that Sydney still had not even glanced my way. Winnie was shaking her head apologetically, with a shrug and head shake toward Sydney. "Don't worry, I'll try again another day."

I found a new seat a few tables over from them, baffled over this girl's behavior. From my new seat among some enchanted freshman girls, I could see that Sydney was now much more relaxed, even though she and Winnie seemed to be arguing a bit over something. I had to ask the girl nearest me, "Do you know her?"

The girl giggled and said, "Not really, but I think she wrote the play. She's kind of weird. He-he-he."

As fun as my new table companions were, I decided to excuse myself and take advantage of a different, emptier table to do some catch-up reading for my new classes. At least that's what I claimed. This table was also closer to Sydney's. Conveniently, I could now eavesdrop on her and Winnie. I really did take out *The Scarlet Letter* to be industrious and decidedly un-creepy. But I couldn't help it that I could hear them loud and clear.

Any argument they might have been having about me and my former presence at their table seemed to be quite finished. Now they were talking about books. It seemed that Sydney was applauding the fact that Winnie had taken to reading something that wasn't a fashion magazine or social media. But then Sydney took the book from her, eager to see what it was.

"Holy crap, Winnie! You can't read this. Are you kidding me?"

Winnie snatched it back. "What the hell, judgy? It's a book. You should be doing your little literacy jig. Go Winnie. You so smart."

Sydney took the book back, seemingly for the sole purpose of gesturing at it in disgust. "No, this is almost straight-up porn."

"It is not! There's tons of parts in there that are like totally not even that sexy."

A challenging pause from Sydney. "Like what?"

"Like I don't know. You read it if you're so curious. It's just a romance."

"But that's the thing. It's not romance at all! There's no love, no beauty of a slowly blooming relationship that's full of hardship but triumphs against all odds. This is just—just smutty descriptions of a couple doing it, then breaking up, then doing it again, and so on . . ."

"Yeah, yeah, yeah. Not up to the Sydney Camden standards."

Winnie didn't even think to accuse Sydney of hating it because it reminded her of the Josh disaster, and Sydney sure wasn't going to bring up any thoughts about the incident that their conversation might be sparking.

Winnie made a grab to get her book back from her friend as Sydney smugly tossed the thing like a basketball into a nearby trash can. Winnie rolled her eyes. "Whatever. Took too much brain power anyway."

The bell rang. Everyone around me started to hop up, and I sat there motionless. Because I suddenly gave absolutely zero cares about the various circumstances hinting she was not for me to pursue. I knew I had stumbled upon my dream girl.

⸻

So the next day, I had to try again.

I waited patiently until lunch and then once more casually approached their table. I decided to play it as if she hadn't given me an absurdly cold shoulder yesterday, as if there was no reason for me not to sit with them.

"Is it just me, or is the general population of this school a bit on the unfriendly side?" I said as I pulled out a chair and planted myself. "I don't typically have much trouble making friends, but so far about the friendliest people I've come across were the table of freshman girls I sat with after leaving you two yesterday. And I'd say they were a bit *too* friendly, if you get me. Fourteen to seventeen's a rather awkward age gap, wouldn't you think?" I smiled. No reason not to treat these two as if they were my best chums in the world.

Winnie smiled ditzily at me. Flirty-laughed. "You're funny."

Awkward. I wanted to share a laugh with Sydney over it,

and for some reason intuited that her personality was one that could meet me halfway to share the joke. In normal circumstances, I would have been right. But now, I looked to her and found her still looking as decidedly away from me as yesterday. Only, she was staring daggers at Winnie. Winnie was oblivious to this. So Sydney did her best to remedy that by giving her a kick to the shin.

Or trying to. In fact, she actually kicked *me* in the shin. I jumped and rubbed my shin, and she slowly glanced up in embarrassed horror, as I said, "I must say, we really are much more welcoming in England."

And our eyes met.

The magic of it ended just as quickly, as she dropped her glance back to the table, muttering, "Sorry."

Before I had a chance to try another joke or say something amazingly sweet and sensitive to sweep her off her feet, a rather theatrical-looking girl came along, putting a hand comfortingly on Sydney's back. Sydney jumped slightly but relaxed as she saw who it was.

"Hey, girl," she said to Sydney, "the rest of the drama club and I just wanted to let you know how much we appreciate you. This thing with Josh has really made us realize not to take people for granted. Hang in there, hon."

And the girl continued on her way, leaving me staring after, my mind putting the pieces together. "Josh?" I asked slowly.

Winnie replied, "Yeah, Josh. Let's talk about anything else. Like you…"

I ignored her dreamy gaze. "She's…" And I finally put it all together, what I should have figured out much, much sooner. "She's grieving Josh?"

"Um… yeah?" Winnie said, glancing at Sydney.

But Sydney was abruptly pushing her chair back and standing up. Leaving us there without a look back. I only barely registered Winnie saying flirtily, "So you're, like, foreign?"

I stood up. "Terribly sorry, excuse me." And I continued one more step down the rabbit hole of attraction to this girl, thinking only of my horror at what had been done to her and wishing to convey that horror, offer what little comfort or apology I could. If I would have had time to really mull it over and think it through, I probably would have realized that a girl typically doesn't want to talk about a recent sexual assault with a random chap she barely knows, and I probably would have realized that her behavior toward me thus far was good indication that I should let her be just then rather than let her in on the fact that I knew her secret. However, I didn't have such time to mull it over, and instead I felt compelled by my emotional attachment and my above-mentioned horror to go ahead and stupidly follow her.

I found her outside, sitting on the grass and writing furiously in a notebook.

At the sound of my footfalls, she glanced and then jumped up. And she almost started to back away from me again as she had at the party, but she stopped herself. Instead, she scowled at me.

I gave it a go. "Sydney? I'm sorry. I had no idea."

"No idea about what?"

"That Josh—erm, I'm his cousin, and I know what he did, I just didn't know that it was you ..."

And now she really did take a step back from me, as if I might be contaminated because of my blood relationship to the fellow.

But instead of dissolving into terror like she nearly

appeared to be considering, she stuck with the scowl. "Come on, then. Let's get this over with."

I only stared at her like a dolt, oblivious to what she could possibly be talking about.

She continued. "Well what about it? Are you here to mock me over it? Maybe tell me what a terrible person I am for letting everyone think—"

I interrupted her. "What? No, no! Drat, what a buggered situation, this. I'm so sorry. I—"

"You're so sorry? And then, oops, you'll make me a laughingstock again? Maybe—maybe rape me, too?"

Horrified, I cried, "No! I only—"

"Then leave me the hell alone." And she turned and walked away.

I stared after her in horror, finally beginning to understand what kind of mess I had walked into.

—

Sydney had to cope, which means she went back to her notebook once again. This time, she was more frantic than ever, desperate to make her confusion and humiliation go away, as she poured out her heart and her wishes into the pages that night.

Today, a man attacked me, she wrote.

What? Who attacked you? Wait for it . . . it was me. How, you ask? Like this:

Sydney rewrote the scene of her and me from earlier. In it, I looked like me physically, but for all intents and purposes, I might as well have been Josh. For fake me was looking at her lustfully, shoving her up against a wall. *I fought back,* she wrote. And she shoved me viciously. We struggled, and she slapped me hard across the face. But it didn't stop me. She gave me a fierce knee to the groin—that stopped me. I doubled over in pain. *I defended myself against him.* And she stood triumphant, strong, reveling in my pain.

She kept writing: Moments later, I was shoved into the back of a cop car as she stood with her head held high among the crowd of gawking students.

Sydney felt satisfied with the scene, but there was a problem, a plot problem with the story she'd created. If this were really the way it had gone down, as she half-believed/half-hoped/half-deluded herself into thinking, then what could explain the fact that she would still inevitably see me around in real life? She gave the matter some thought for a moment and then concluded, *I don't have to worry anymore. Because even if I see him again, if perhaps he gets out on bail, it won't matter. Because I have the power now. Everyone knows what he's done, so I will be safe.*

And thus did she transfer and transform all the animosity, fear, and hatred that she could hardly acknowledge for her real attacker when she was going around pretending to mourn him. She transformed it into a superior victory, and she transferred the ill-feelings to a new object.

To me.

11

WINNIE WAS ALL BUT dying for details from her reticent friend by the time they entered school the next morning, after a commute full of Sydney skillfully steering their conversation in other distracting directions. At long last, Winnie broke in, "Syd, hold up and tell me what happened yesterday! With Mr. British Hottie?" Sydney only shrugged. "At lunch? Come on, I'm dying here."

Sydney sighed and said carefully, "I don't have to worry about him anymore."

"Why? Details, woman!"

Sydney took her time answering, noticing vaguely as they walked that the balance at school truly seemed to have shifted—greetings, nods, waves coming her way from every direction, not one tinged with mockery or malice. "Okay, here's what happened. He . . . he came at me. Like attacked me? And I fought back."

To which Winnie exclaimed, "Holy crap, yeah you did! Tell me how you're such a magnet for this stuff! Wow. So now what?"

"Now . . . I don't have to be afraid of him anymore?" This was her vague answer. And it seemed to satisfy Winnie.

That was basically all they said on the matter, how she left things on the information front with Winnie. And not that I can terribly blame Sydney at this messed-up point in her life, but let's be honest, it was basically a disaster waiting to happen for my reputation as a nice or even tolerable guy.

And this is also about when they rounded the corner and saw me. Of course, I knew nothing just then of their conversation's contents. So I had no real idea why they were both walking past me with their heads held high and gazes averted, when yesterday I would have at least expected to count on the fact that Winnie would be goofily friendly toward me.

I watched them, a little puzzled but mostly wearing the usual obviously wistful look on my face. And I was startled by a voice nearby me saying, "Trust me, you don't want to go there."

I turned to see the very same Kendall girl who'd been tipsily doing her best to flirt with me at that terrible party. I had seen her in the hallway yesterday, briefly considered that the smile and wave she was doing might be directed at me, and then promptly forgot about her. For she was rather forgettable, in a cookie-cutter/overdone/supermodel wannabe type of way. And here she was again, leaning in conspiratorially by my shoulder, as if the two of us were best mates. With benefits.

"Hmm?" I asked, scooching a little away from her.

"Sydney Camden. Total space cadet freak."

I frowned at this, and I began walking away, telling her over my shoulder, "Don't believe I asked you for a review."

She took no hint and fell into step beside me. "I've known

her forever. She's a total goody-two shoes, walks around in her own world, sucks up to all the teachers ..."

And, curse my luck, the more this irritating girl rambled on about the things wrong with Sydney, the more I fell for Sydney. Frustrating.

Eventually the class bell forced this Kendall to part ways from me, and I breathed a sigh of relief on that front but was concerned on another: I was beginning to realize that this situation of my growing attraction to Sydney warranted some more definite action on my part. I now knew that Sydney was a struggling, confused rape victim, and she had asked me to leave her the hell alone. That meant that now was probably a good time for me to enter into full-distraction mode so I could faithfully do as she'd asked. What was my endgame in this endeavor? Well I certainly had hopes that with time she might heal a bit and become a little less hostile toward me, enough that I might somehow sweep her off her feet as I seemed to do without even trying to all the Kendalls in the world.

But all in good time. For now, I had one task: getting my mind off Sydney.

So that evening, I decided once again to utilize exercise as a means to vent my frustrations. I threw on some casual clothes and jumped onto my bike. Which was a marvelous plan. Not.

That phenomenon that some people insist on calling "coincidence" really can be a funny thing, enough to convince former skeptics of a fate or an all-knowing Providence, I would think. Because here is where I finally realized that I lived a mere two streets over from Sydney.

I was riding along obliviously, wondering how long or hard I would need to ride to actually feel like I was exerting myself, when who should I see but Sydney out in her front lawn. She was sitting in her nest of books and notebooks, and tonight Winnie was there studying with her.

Winnie saw me first. "Don't. Look. Up."

Of course Sydney instantly looked up. And laid her eyes on me as I stared in dumb shock riding past them.

Winnie was quickly hopping up, giving me the finger and yelling, "Screw off, perv!"

Eek, I thought, peddling away faster and hoping I somehow looked as casual and non-stalker-like as I was in reality to any bystanders who might be observing this interaction.

What I didn't know was that behind me, Sydney was pulling Winnie back down, glancing anxiously toward the house, where Maryanne was at the kitchen window, looking out with confusion as she made dinner.

Sydney was absurdly hoping that somehow her mother had not seen it, or even more absurdly that she would say nothing about it.

Things didn't look promising on that front, as Maryanne immediately called them in for dinner.

Sydney gathered her books quickly, madly trying to think of explanations, excuses, stories, anything. Which was a difficult task, as her brain was becoming more muddled by the moment on just why it was that she and Winnie now had this outward, apparently real conflict with me when I had not really done anything to her … or had I?

Once she was inside, she saw immediately by Maryanne's exaggerated casualness that questions were coming. And sure enough, her mother exercised the self-control to allow about forty-five seconds to elapse, before: "Girls … who was that boy that drove by on his bike out there?"

Sydney was trying to covertly shake her head in warning at Winnie behind Maryanne's back. But Winnie was oblivious to this and instead blurted it all out, just in time for Robert to enter and hear as well. "Oh don't get us started on Calvin! That d-bag like came at Sydney, but don't worry, she was all—"

It was at this point that Sydney more or less covered Winnie's mouth. Winnie twisted to look at her, confused, while her parents whipped around to stare in shock. "In my story!" Sydney spat out. "I based a character off that guy, in a story I'm working on. I don't really know him. Winnie's confused. We'll be back in a sec. Winnie, why don't I just let you read it?"

And she pulled Winnie up the stairs with her, leaving her parents behind her with puzzled looks. "Should we be concerned?" Maryanne asked. "Is she too wrapped up in her stories?"

Robert glanced after them, a little disturbed himself, which was something. "Possibly . . ." But there was little to do about it in the then and there, if that was the case. So the two of them left it disturbingly at that.

Up in Sydney's room, Sydney was doing her best to satisfactorily explain matters to Winnie, while writing more at the same time.

But Winnie was saying, "Now I'm extra lost. Did it happen, or didn't it?"

Sydney was too concerned with another matter to care much about Winnie's confusion. "He saw us, right? He knows where I live?"

And suddenly, Winnie had a moment of insight. "This is really terrible for you, isn't it? Like a rerun of Josh?"

But Sydney was too busy writing. *He doesn't know where*

I live. He doesn't know. He wants to leave me alone forever. She wanted the words to comfort her, make everything okay. But it wasn't quite working.

"Syd?" Winnie broke in.

"Yeah, no. I'm fine. Let's go eat."

—

Meanwhile, I was rapidly discarding any notion of partaking in outdoor leisure activities in the neighborhood, and I turned to other means of distraction.

First, in the home. Or that is, the place where I dwelled, anyway.

Despite the tragedy that had rocked the household, no one seemed the least bit more connected or together in any way. If anything, they seemed more distant than ever as they coped in their separate ways.

Strangely enough, I was perhaps least concerned about my often-weeping aunt. I got the feeling that she was handling it in a way that was normal for her, as excruciating as it was. Uncle Sal was, well … I'd get back to this grump of the house eventually, I supposed. I really hadn't the foggiest idea of what he might have needed, and I had a suspicion that I was not the one to offer it to him anyway. But my particular concern just then was Pam.

Considering that she did already seem to tend toward the dark and depressing things of life, her brother's death and confession to her had only seemed to increase her dreariness in the few days that had passed. I still rarely saw her interacting with the family at all, and she never had any friends over that I knew of. She spent a lot of time in her room alone, listening to depressing music and doing who knows what else.

So one evening I decided to knock again, thinking perhaps we could relive our short spurt of bonding from the other night. But I was met with more of the depressing music and not a sound from her. I knocked again, nothing. Hoping I wasn't about to destroy my slim chances of connecting further, I slowly turned the knob and cracked it just a smidge.

"Pam? Are you decent?"

She was sitting on the bed, holding a razor testingly toward her arm.

She jumped and screamed, "What!" tossing the razor behind her as if I might not have seen it. For my part, my stomach dropped out of my bum, while I did my best not to show my shock.

I cautiously stepped inside and shut the door behind me. "So . . ."

"So what? What do you want? Leave me alone, okay?"

I took a seat at her desk chair. "Well, you see, I could try that, but now I must admit I'm rather frightened you'd chop your arm clean off by the end of the night."

She didn't find the humor, stared stone-faced back at me. "Leave me alone. Like everyone else does."

I decided to drastically change gears, to shake her out of her misery. "Want to have a listen to my problems?"

"No."

"I figured. But I'm going to tell you anyway. We're both bloody miserable, from what I can figure out, so we might as well bitch about it together for a bit."

"Oh, did your dip-shit brother dump his rape-guilt on you mere minutes before croaking too?"

"No, it's just that my mother died and sent me to live with relative-strangers in a foreign country, none of whom seem to like me much. And that mere days after arriving, I fell for a girl I hadn't met yet when I saw her at a funeral for a cousin I never got to know but soon learned many unpleasant things about. And that—"

"Aw, you fell in love with someone? Poor you. My heart breaks for you."

"Oh but it will. It's Sydney."

"Huh?"

"I didn't know who in the bloody hell she was. I just felt terribly attracted to her for no apparent reason, tried to start pursuing her, stumbled onto—well, the truth. And now she knows I know and quite thoroughly seems to hate me. So there we are."

Pam was silent for a moment. "Oh."

I nodded. "Would you give me the razor?"

She looked mildly alarmed. "Don't you start cutting."

"Nor you."

"I wasn't really going to," she said quietly, reaching behind her to hand me the razor.

A likely story. I knew she was lying by the fact that she was willingly surrendering it to me. She didn't want to start down this destructive road, as compelling it might have seemed to her as she sat here alone mere minutes ago. And once again, I marveled at what some would call a coincidence of timing.

All I said, though, as I took the razor from her, was, "Would you talk to someone?"

"You mean like a shrink? Don't push it."

Precisely. It seemed there was no pushing things with this

wannabe tough girl. So I said, "Will you come talk to me when you need to?"

"You just said yourself about all the crap you're dealing with right now."

"Trust me, helping with yours would actually very much distract me from mine. A win-win."

After a moment, she shrugged and muttered, "Maybe..." in a manner that said, "Conversation over, please." So I took the hint and turned to leave, heartened despite her hard front and her harder issues, because it did feel like a very real possibility of helping her through some of them.

—

After that connection with Pam, I was optimistic. Crazily enough, I was thinking that I'd be able to somehow connect the whole family to each other in addition to me.

But as I stood at the crossroads between Uncle Sal in his den and Aunt Jem in the kitchen the next evening, I knew it would probably not be that easy.

I decided to start small and took the non-intimidating route. Aunt Jem had a laptop open on the kitchen table with a bunch of bills and invoices spread around her. She was very intent but looking rather distressed. I considered offering to help her, but financials were hardly my strong suit. So instead, I went to the mound of dishes in the sink and started cleaning them without a word.

I didn't realize that she was watching me, first with confusion as if no one had ever helped her with the dishes before, and then with tears. Her sob startled me, because her trying to smother it really only served to make the sound more alarming. "Sorry," she was saying, "You must think I'm such a silly fountain by now."

I laughed a little as I hurriedly dried my hands and went to hug her. All my aunt really seemed to need right now was someone to hold her. That was something I could do.

I thought that perhaps, though it would inevitably end quite differently than it had with Aunt Jem, a bit of material, chore-type help might go a ways with Uncle Sal as well. So the next afternoon I took the liberty of giving his luxury sedan a good wash in the driveway.

I realized halfway through that he was watching from the window. I gave him a chipper wave. And I was met with a disgusted head-shake, as Uncle Sal mouthed something that looked an awful lot like, "Freak."

Oh. Well that's discouraging. I tried not to let it get me down too terribly, and I plotted my next move in mission distraction.

It was at this point in my quest for distraction that I returned once again to that certain, unremarkable-looking building I had passed during my first sight-seeing Saturday here in Seattle. It being Saturday again, I expected, rightly, to find a similar crowd gathered outside it once more.

With a bit more time and distance, now, since my mother's death, I thought myself quite able to dive into this activity. But, though I had never in the past had any remarkable difficulty adapting to new people and situations, I found myself veritably swimming in awkwardness as I approached.

The same sweet, curly-haired old woman was here, along with a half-dozen or so other unremarkable people, and I strode up to them with exaggerated assurance of myself. And then she turned the full force of her sweet smile on me.

"Hi there, dear. How are you this afternoon?"

It shouldn't have meant a thing, truly. But the smile, the love—I felt suddenly like I had found my grandmother! I hadn't realized until that moment how starving for even an ounce of affection I'd been these past weeks, how utterly alone I had felt. And perhaps it still hadn't been so very long or far since my mother's passing. For whatever the reason, I felt tears gather in my eyes. Bugger it all, I couldn't do it.

With an apologetic smile, I turned to leave. But she scurried forward and gently grabbed my arm. "What is it, honey?"

And suddenly, a bunch of things seemed to happen at once. I turned back toward her. I tried to wipe the tears out of my eyes and look sane. The rest of the group kept up their quiet praying. And the door to the building burst open as a female security guard came rushing out.

In her late 20s, tall and tough but still feminine, this woman imposingly addressed my new elderly friend: "Dorothy! Hands off the customers! Don't make me call you in."

Dorothy dropped her hand from my arm with the kind of discreet eye-roll that can only look endearing on a ninety-year-old, while the security guard advanced toward me.

"Sorry about that, sir," she was saying to me. I saw her name tag read *Tatiana*. And she was trying to direct me toward the building. "I can escort you back inside."

I practically jumped as I realized she thought *I* was a customer. I took a step back. "I wasn't in there!"

"Oh," she said. Tight smile. "Sorry." And she shook her head, stalking back inside.

Dorothy and I looked at one another. In another time and place, I would have spat out a joke about the woman having mistaken me for some other handsome devil. But right now, all I could do was laugh, in a mirth teetering on grief. Dorothy smiled back at me as I carried on. "The irony! My mum nearly had me done in for in one of those." And I laughed some more, until it turned thoroughly to tears. First laughing tears, then real ones. And before I knew it, Dorothy had me sitting on the curb bawling like a baby against her, while I poured out my bloody tale of woe to the first legitimate friend/surrogate grandmother I had found in Seattle.

⸺

Thus I found a new pastime. Yes, I was aware that I was falling into an unthanked, irritating group of people that much of society disapproved of, or considered to be busybodies—get your rosaries off my ovaries and all that. And who was I but some cloddish fellow who could know nothing of what a woman was really going through when she turned to such a thing? Perhaps I couldn't, but surely I did know *something* of it, given my past. And now I finally felt that I could take that something and put it to good, to giving some bit of help.

So the next Saturday I was back, this time arriving before the others. I'd been given helpful pamphlets and a sign last week, and so I thought I was ready when I saw a rather scared-looking young woman approaching from the parking lot out back.

She was avoiding eye contact with me, definitively not looking at the sign I held that read, "Abortion stops a beating heart." I took a step into her sight line and greeted her. "Hello there."

Briskly, she pointed to my sign. "I'm not going in there for that."

I fell into step beside her as she walked toward the clinic. "Oh what a relief. That would be a tough spot to be in if you were." I pulled out a pamphlet. "I've got these for people who *are*, because I don't think they realize there are all these other places that want to help them. Maybe you know someone…"

And hesitantly, she took a pamphlet, pretending not to read it.

I realized we were rather near the door, just didn't realize how near. Until my good friend Tatiana burst out of it. "Excuse me, you are *over* the property line."

I glanced at my feet to see that I was indeed no longer on the public sidewalk, by a few inches. I hopped back to the proper side as she then ushered my scared young acquaintance inside.

A brief moment later, Tatiana was back, alone. She crossed her arms, staring me down. I smiled. "Sorry about that. New in town."

"Not that new. I saw you last week." A pause. I didn't feel the urge to fill it. "I don't take any shit," she told me.

"Wouldn't dream of giving you any."

"I should probably call the cops on you for trespassing."

"Because my life isn't bloody awful enough," I replied cheerily.

She eyed me up and down. "Are you over eighteen?"

"Does it matter?" I asked warily.

She rolled her eyes. "Guess that means no. Give me your parents' phone number and I won't call the cops. This time."

"Oh I'm an orphan."

And thus it came to transpire that, a matter of minutes later, I found myself speeding away in the passenger side of Uncle Sal's (very clean) luxury sedan while his surly attitude confirmed my suspicion that I was now officially on his bad side.

Lovely. Like I really needed the one father figure who was legitimately present in my life to all but hate me.

I tried to budge him a bit. "I wasn't intending to cause trouble." No response. "It's not like I was out and about trying to do some . . . rabble-rousing?" I said it in my best American accent. And I got nothing.

I gave it some thought for a moment. What was the angle to take with him? I'd been thinking, recently, about the fact that Josh had been almost the same age as me, and our mothers twins. I knew little of whether Jem's circumstances were identical to what my mother's had been, but Jem and Sal obviously hadn't been married yet at seventeen when Josh was conceived, so I had to assume their situation was somewhat similar to my mother's. I decided to appeal to Sal's past experiences now. "Surely we're on the same side of the issue, I presume? Considering Josh being born—"

He cut me off quickly. "Don't speak to me about Josh. We did what was best for us and I'd appreciate you not sticking your nose into our business. I *would* show you the same courtesy, if I weren't getting calls like this to force me into your business."

Well then. I didn't have a response. We rode the rest of the way in silence, and I mentally crossed out any possibility of finding a type of surrogate father in this fellow.

So naturally, the next course of action to my distraction-seeking mind was to set back about the task of tracking down my real father once again. Because obviously, despite my words to Tatiana, I wasn't in fact an orphan. The various significant events of the past few weeks had kept me from pursuing what I'd thought would be my primary focus here in the States. And if ever I needed as much family as I could get my hands on, so to speak, now was that time.

Upon arriving at home, with the silent treatment continuing, I excused myself and took to the internet. My phone was rather bottom-of-the-line slow, and I quickly became frustrated. Glancing around the pit-room, my eyes fell on Josh's laptop.

It felt wrong to consider using a dead guy's laptop . . . for a second. Then I decided he certainly had no use for it anymore and was probably a lot more concerned with his present uncomfortable circumstances—erm, in Purgatory, where I hoped him to be. At any rate, he could hardly mind, so I opened it up.

And . . . password protected. Drat.

I put in some random letters to get the hint. It read, "Hint: Me." Hmm. I tried his name a couple ways, no go. What else? "Cool guy"? "Hot stuff?" "Stud muffin?" Nothing along those lines worked.

I was nearly ready to give up when I realized Pam was standing in the doorway behind me. "Didn't you read the hint?" she asked.

"Me," I replied. "What's it mean?"

"Me. That's his password. M-e."

"Ohhhh." I quickly typed it in, feeling dense. "Here I was trying his name and things like 'sports god.'"

"Watch out, though. There's probably a crap-load of porn on there. I think it's even saved to the desktop."

I paused visibly.

"I figured you were the type to mind."

I felt like pursuing this. "How'd you guess that?"

She shrugged. "I don't know. You're just very different

from …" She motioned her head room-ward, as if the leftover refuse served to symbolize all that there was of her brother.

I pondered a moment, considering how carefully to tread—and then decided I might not ever get as good an opening as this. "Are you worried? About him?"

"*Now?* Seems like the time for that is past, right?" She didn't look like this was exactly a thrilling topic for her, and yet she inched inside a little, around the crap, to sit.

"No, I mean, you know, his afterlife …"

"What's the point? If there is a God, don't you think a rapist is probably pretty fair game for eternal damnation?"

I cringed. She didn't. Goodness, it seemed she really did hate him.

"No … I mean …" I thought for a moment, and settled on a firm, "Yes, but." She waited for me to go on. "You told me he said he hoped he didn't go to hell, right?"

"Well yeah, but I mean holy crap dude, good luck with that. Don't you think?"

I shook my head. "Obviously we can't know anything for sure until we kick the bucket ourselves, but my understanding is that a fellow's got to be totally unrepentant to go to hell. So hoping you're not headed downward is probably enough for God to work with. It's not really my call, but gun to my head if I had to guess, I'd wager Josh is just in for a particularly harsh Purgatory about now."

She mulled that over. "Huh. Well I guess God must be a lot more forgiving than me."

"That's the idea."

Clearly wanting to change the subject, she motioned for

me to hand her the laptop. "Give it here." I complied. She did some clicking for a few moments. "Can't guarantee that's all of it, but I deleted the porn off the desktop anyway."

"Thanks!"

She got up to leave. "Don't mention it."

Well that felt better. I'd been wanting to say something like that to her for days now.

I got back to my task. Thomas Tucker.

Of course an online search brought ten billion results, including an actor and a realty firm. Neither of those people were near the right age to be my father, though.

I found a people search engine and a listing of addresses. This database had fifty-two Thomas Tuckers with addresses in the States. No saying any of them were actually my dad. I wasn't quite sure how to narrow it down further.

But what did I have to lose? On impulse, I dialed the first number.

An old and grumpy sounding female voice answered on the first ring. "Yes, hello there," I responded. "I'm looking for Thomas Tucker. I think he might be my father."

"He's dead," was the blunt reply.

"Sorry?"

"He was ninety-six, and definitely not your father." Click.

Oh. Well, what did I expect? And yet, the silence on the other end of the line was so discouraging that I didn't have the heart to try another.

12

WHILE I WAS ATTEMPTING all these distraction tactics with varying levels of success, Sydney was meanwhile learning slowly how to cope, in a way. Of course she didn't realize it, but this particular way of hers—denial and pretending that everything was a-okay—was not going to hold up. For now, though, she was doing all right. And I could tell, from my vantage point of as far away from her as possible. She seemed to be coming in to her own as a respectable member of the student body. Whether this was because her classmates felt too guilty to torment her or had actually come to a realization of what an amazing person she was, or both, wasn't important. What mattered was that she was doing okay, outwardly anyway.

For my part, I continued on in the unsatisfying task of avoiding her. Most people probably would have concluded that neither of us knew the other existed, but that would have been entirely false as we both went about our days in purposeful avoidance of one another, for two very different reasons.

But this separation of ours was not destined to last, and the path of our fates joining once again started one morning some four weeks after we first met, with the occasion of my becoming covered in vomit.

I was at my locker, aware that Sydney was passing behind me, and doing my darnedest to avoid gazing wistfully after her. But I could see her in my peripherals. And she looked terrible.

My instinct was to follow, investigate, see if she was all right. But I checked myself. Stopped, undecided. Looked at her. Goodness did she look green.

And before I knew what had happened, our paths had crossed. She stopped. I stopped. We locked eyes.

I was about to ask, offer help. When she gagged violently and vomited literally down the front of me.

She wiped her mouth and gazed up at me in horror. Despite the stench, I could only smile. "Feel better?"

"I covered you in my vomit."

"It'll wash. Do you need help? Walk you to the nurse?" She shook her head no, glancing around, desperation starting to set in. She could hardly stand here talking to her imagined attacker, clear object of righteous anger, and guy she definitely was *not* romantically attracted to. I offered, "Shall I fetch you Winnie?" And she glanced up at me, fighting with herself. But the truth of the matter was that she felt bloody awful physically. So, looking away as if she were ashamed of herself, she nodded. And then ran off into the nearest bathroom.

I located Winnie without too much difficulty and sent her in, I having no idea of the conversation that was about to follow between the two of them.

Winnie found her pacing in front of the stalls, still green, holding a notebook she'd just written in, and muttering, "I'm not sick, I'm not sick, I'm not sick . . ." In this instance, after all, there was no messing around. Sydney had gotten right to the task of denial and pretending. But of course, it was not working.

Winnie pulled up short. "What's wrong? Are you like dying, to send *Calvin* after me like that?" No answer. "What, you're puking? You have the flu? Calvin didn't do something to you, did he?"

Now Sydney stopped pacing. Stared at her. Shook her head no. Winnie stared back. "Well what, then?"

Sydney glanced back at the stalls. All empty. Still, she felt the need to only whisper the words, straight into Winnie's ear.

Winnie practically jumped into the air. "What!"

"Don't say it, don't say it out loud. It can't be real, right? That's not what this is?"

"Oh totally. Stop freaking. You're puking from some gnarly PMS and your period will be here by lunch time." They stared at one another for a beat, neither of them believing Winnie's words.

Winnie grabbed Sydney's hand and pulled her toward the door. "We're ditching this morning."

You know it had to be a huge problem by the fact that Sydney did not protest at this suggestion but went along without a peep.

The fifteen minutes round trip that it took the two of them to drive to a mini-mart and back, but most especially the four of those minutes during which Sydney sat in Winnie's car while Winnie bravely went inside to purchase a home pregnancy test, seemed to last an eternity.

But that was nothing compared to the two minutes Sydney had to wait, staring at the urine stick and watching two pink lines appear in all their glory.

Winnie was outside the stall, leaning against the sinks, picking at her nail polish. "'Kay it's totally been two minutes now. Just read it."

An unnecessary prompting. Sydney was already bursting out of the stall, washing her hands, as if she could wash it all away.

Winnie looked at her expectantly. "Well?"

Lips closed, Sydney shook her head. Winnie, unsure what to take that as, asked, "No?" Sydney only shook her head again. "No, it's not no? What, woman?"

Still, Sydney didn't speak. She briskly dried her hands and ripped open her backpack for her notebook. And she leaned against the counter beside Winnie, scribbling away.

"Syd, come on. Say something. Are you gonna make me dig through the tampon trash to find it and read it myself?"

Sydney was still writing. Without looking up, she said, "I can fix this . . ."

"Ohhhhhkay . . . So it was positive then?"

"I'm fixing it!"

Winnie watched her with confusion, and she started to become concerned. This wasn't like Sydney. Lately, a lot of Sydney's behavior hadn't been like Sydney. And Winnie, while understanding at least somewhat the cause of this, was beginning to get rather sick of it all.

But now was clearly not the time to leave Sydney hanging. She gently tried to pull the notebook out of Sydney's hands. "You can't fix it in there, Syd. You just can't."

Now Sydney looked up, her eyes desperate. "I *have* to. Because, if I can't . . . then it's over."

"What's over?"

Sydney slowly slid to the floor, her despair beginning to mount. "Everything. What people think about me and Josh, what I . . ." It was too complicated to put it all into words, the elaborate deception she was trying to hide inside. Instead, she summarized, "The moment they find out, I go back to being Sydney the freak, only even worse now."

Winnie sat down beside her. "Hey, no. I'm not letting that happen, okay? We'll fix this. Just not in your notebook."

"But how?"

"You can get an abor—"

In one quick movement, Sydney's hand shot to Winnie's mouth, covering it. And Sydney found herself looking to every corner of the room as if the spiders and the toilet paper dust were going to overhear. "Are you crazy?" she whispered frantically. "You can't say that here!" Sydney might not have been quite solid on all the ins and outs of Catholic moral teaching, but abortion being a no-no was a pretty obvious one.

Winnie sighed and rolled her eyes. "Oh come on. Big Catholic school, oh no. Like we're not all screwing each other and on the pill and watching our parents get divorced? Nobody cares about that stuff anymore. It's not a big deal."

Sydney tried to believe this, to let the nearly reassuring words sink into her psyche. But instead, she said slowly, "But it's supposed to be a big deal, right?"

Winnie shrugged. "You're also a girl in a shitty situation. That's all that really matters."

Sydney closed her eyes, trying to calm her speeding heart rate. "Tell me none of this is real."

"Well, right now it is. But I'll help you figure out how to make it so it's not real anymore, okay? I think we can do that."

Sydney nodded. But she wasn't sure she believed it, any more than she was sure she believed everything else she'd been pretending the past few weeks.

———

Normally, Sydney could go through an entire school day without once entertaining thoughts related to the religious affiliation of her school. Except for the one semester she had had to take a theology class, the only reminder she normally had of the school's Catholicism was the fact that they all went around in those spiffy uniforms.

But today, the one day in her life when she had ever wanted to fully forget it, she was somehow bombarded with constant reminders that she walked the halls of a Catholic school.

Between classes, it was a crucifix staring at her from a wall in the hallway where she had never noticed it before. She turned her head to avoid looking at it and instead found herself face to face with the huge statue of the school's namesake, St. Aloysius Gonzaga, a pious-looking priest who seemed to be looking her straight in the eye. So Sydney dropped her gaze, quickened her pace. Rounded a corner, and here was a large sign on a door that announced EUCHA-RISTIC CHAPEL with a stick-figure guy kneeling. She gave the room a huge berth and continued on.

As if these encounters weren't jarring enough to her frazzled psyche, she slipped into class a few moments later and found herself facing a huge vocations poster on the wall with a big picture of a nun on it. Sydney actually jumped as a, "Gah!" slipped out of her mouth. Realizing she'd said it aloud, she glanced around but found that no one seemed to have noticed in the pre-class chatter.

So she took her seat and got out her notebook. To try to write, try to block out the world, try to change the way of things so that Winnie's words could be true, so that Sydney could actually believe that no one cared, and that the values and morals and rules she'd been brought up in were of no consequence.

But by the end of the school day, after hours of such unfruitful mental exercises, she was about to crack.

She needed to get out, through the suffocating crowds, escape the religion that she felt chasing her. In her mind, there were priests, nuns, rosaries, incense, candles, religious symbols and figures everywhere, all staring at her, chasing her even, as she tried to repeat to herself a mantra of non-consequence, a belief that none of it mattered. That no one cared, least of all the distant, amorphous God of Catholicism, who seemed completely absent from her current misery.

She was oblivious to me as I watched her from the sidelines, saw her hurrying out of there as if all of hell was after her. And she was even more oblivious to the real priest who was standing behind me, watching me watch her, there almost as if to disprove her feelings of Divine abandonment. But he only said to me, "Is she okay?"

I turned and saw him there. "I'm not sure."

He replied, "You might want to check into it, if she's someone you care about."

I nodded and walked away, contemplating how best to proceed in doing so when she wished me to leave her the hell alone.

I'll be the first to admit that I'm not always the quickest to pick up on happenings that are obvious to some more intuitive people. So despite the vomit, and the timing of the vomit, I remained oblivious to the new terrible development in Sydney's issue-filled existence. But I couldn't stop thinking about the ominous, near-detonation look about her as she'd left, a look that told me so clearly how wrong things were with her. I wanted to follow the advice of the priest, but I felt I couldn't. Even practically speaking, I had no simple way to do so, as it was Friday and I wouldn't see her until school again on Monday. I sighed. It was going to be one long weekend.

But as I walked my bike out streetward to head home, I had a small eureka. Or, more accurately, I had a moment of keen observation and realized that her play was opening that night. How had I not noticed these banners before? This was marvelous!

I hopped on my bike but didn't peddle home. Rather, I circled around searching for Pam. Moments later, I spotted her, walking alone out from the quad.

"Pam!" I called, my excitement probably seeming bizarrely disproportionate to my bleak surroundings. She looked startled. I toned it down a notch and asked, "Do you have plans tonight?"

"Take a guess," she responded rather sullenly.

"Want to come see Sydney's play with me?" She paused, as if about to say no. "Please?" I turned on the charm with a big smile.

"That's just creepy, and not convincing me."

"My treat?"

With a sigh: "I guess."

"Fantastic!"

And it was. But more on that in a moment.

First, a look at Sydney's night.

Of course, as the playwright, she had to attend. But if she could have escaped it without drawing more attention to herself, she would have.

Especially considering the events of her school day, Sydney wanted nothing more than to stay home and curl up with a book. She could certainly play the sick card to make an excuse to her parents, but her newly-elevated-from-sub-human status at school meant there were other people to think of. If she didn't show, her classmates would speculate, wonder, gossip about her. All things she very much did not want. The drama people were even expecting her to come out on stage for the bows at the end, a prospect that originally had frightened her nearly to a non-pregnant vomit. But at least, ever since all that had gone down, she didn't really have to fear that someone might throw a produce item or something at her anymore.

And so, social pressure winning out, she put up with her mother's hovering excitement, her father's cold-but-probably-proud demeanor, and Winnie's ditsy questions about the plot throughout the whole production. She sat through the agony of watching the audience, hoping they loved it, watching the actors, hoping they didn't botch it. And when she took her bow on stage at the end, to a pretty decent-sized applause, she finally felt as if her days of being an outcast were over. And it was lovely.

Until a wave of nausea hit her like a cold piece of produce and reminded her that it was to end all too soon if she let things go on in this way.

Of course I had no idea about any of this as I sat there watching and luxuriating in the opportunity to glimpse her lovely soul through her play. It's not too often that one gets a thorough look into the heart of the person he loves. Usually, one must pretty much content himself with everyday conversation and the poor insights it might offer into the inner workings of his beloved's mind . . . Perhaps I lay it on rather thick, but suffice it to say that watching her play was fantastic. Even with mediocre high school performances, it was easy to tell that she was talented.

It was a love story, a tale of misunderstandings and foibles and blunders, of pride and fall, and of fate seeming to play a cruel trick on two people meant to be together. Until, in the end, at long last, love triumphed and the two found their way to one another. It was pure and beautiful. Just as she was.

And high on my happiness at her victory, I felt suddenly emboldened. Hang the whole "leave me the hell alone" line. I was going to talk to her. She could deal and maybe get a clue about how special she was in my eyes.

I said nothing to Pam, and if she noticed any unusual buoyancy about me she didn't betray it in her manner as the two of us made our way through the people to the lobby.

Mostly, people were clumping toward the actors to offer kudos, but there was at least a little crowd near Sydney as well. And I could tell immediately that she wanted out. She looked claustrophobic, rather strangely so. I stopped a moment to observe.

Pam suddenly realized I wasn't beside her. "What up? Why are we stopping? Do we really need more time in this place?" I put my finger to my mouth in a silence motion and nodded toward Sydney. "Ah. More stalking. Great idea."

"Last time I bare the secret blunders of my soul to you," I muttered, for I had told her about my bicycle run-in with

Sydney. Pam crossed her arms impatiently. "Keep your bloody knickers on, I'm just trying to decide if . . ." More like, I was trying to convince myself that it wasn't a bad idea to go talk to her, trying to find any excuse that would make it okay for me to go tell her how splendid I thought her play. When in reality, I knew from the ever-increasing panic in her expression that I needed to stay away.

I sighed, resigning myself. But realized mid-sigh that her bloody parents standing nearby should be noticing her, doing something. They were absently chatting with some other parent, looking at programs, things like that. Until her father looked up at me, as I stood there staring in their direction.

Generally speaking, Robert looked as mild-mannered as he behaved. But just then, as he met eyes with me, there was a subtle change, and I felt inexplicably threatened.

"Okay, let's go," I said to Pam, pulling her quickly toward the exit and wondering how I had managed, in the space of about thirty seconds, to make myself appear practically as sketchy as the version of me that Sydney had written about.

13

IF MY WEEKEND was shaping up to be bleak, Sydney's was
that multiplied.

She'd let Winnie take the lead on the current problem
at the forefront of Sydney's life. And Winnie had been
insisting to her that just getting rid of the problem, if you
will, and letting her life go back to normal was the sensible,
realistic, and sane thing to do. Sydney had finally murmured
assent, and Winnie went ahead and took action, certain that
once Sydney had gotten rid of this whole being pregnant
problem things could legitimately go back to normal.

Before attending the premiere, Sydney had fortified
herself with plenty of writing and imagining that there was
nothing wrong or out of the ordinary in her life. But now,
as she lay awake in bed that night, there was no denying the
harsh reality of what she was considering. Only, she wasn't
really considering it fully. She couldn't.

She lay awake nearly all night, trying to think about her
play, about stories completely unrelated to her life. She tried

reading, and in doing so ruined a couple of good books by giving them horrible associations. And when the morning finally dawned, she was extremely relieved, feeling there was nothing more to it but to put all of this behind her as quickly as possible. Hang guilt, hang what she thought were the proper standards and rules and morals for her to have. She couldn't deal with things like this. They were way above her pay-grade as a seventeen-year-old, she told herself. She even tried to reason God into the equation—if He cared about any of this, He could very well have kept things from getting so tangled in the first place. Right? Right? Yet this reasoning didn't quite sit well with her. And, briefly, she allowed herself to acknowledge that. Which lead to her doing something she hadn't done much of in recent years—making a spontaneous prayer for help.

She had long ago fallen out of this practice, which had been much stronger in her childhood. As she had grown as a writer, her plotting and problem-solving skills had crept into her own life in such a manner that she'd tended to just get her own way out of problems. And certainly she had never seen a very dramatic response to those earlier calls for help, so eventually she had just stopped. But now, in her bleakest hours, the inspiration to do so once again popped up. I say "popped up" because the idea to do so came and went quickly, in about the time it took her to internally utter it: "Then fix this!"

She didn't really expect an explosion of help to come forth, and nothing of the sort did happen. So she decided she simply had to stop thinking about this aspect of the situation entirely. Turn off brain, commencing now. And she got out of bed.

There was no use trying to act natural and eat with her parents. None. She knew she couldn't take it, so she made a quick excuse about meeting up with Winnie early (even though Winnie wouldn't normally even be up on a typical Saturday for a couple hours yet) and made as if to leave, wearing sweats. Of course Maryanne had to ask.

"Why the sweats, sweetie?" Sydney paused, realizing she should have known better. Luckily, her hovering mother inadvertently baled her out. "Are you two going to do some exercising? You know they say it helps your brain activity to be active once in a while! That would be a great idea for you!"

Sydney forced a smile and gave a noncommittal, "Yeah. Bye," noting that her father didn't even look up from his breakfast-time science journal to acknowledge her departure.

She speed-walked the few blocks between Winnie's house and hers, forcing her mind to quiet itself. And she let herself in to Winnie's house with the key under the mat, careful to be quiet and not wake Winnie's night-shift-working mother.

She tiptoed to Winnie's room and startled her awake. "Syd? What the hell, you're like three hours early."

"I know, sorry. I couldn't hang out at home. I'm too wound up."

"Well stop it. Just tell yourself it's not a big deal, because it's not. And . . . maybe take a nap?" This as Winnie snuggled back into her blankies and hoped for some more sleep.

Sydney scoffed. "Yeah right. What else you got?" She went over to Winnie's nearly bookless bookshelf to browse her movies.

Winnie suggested, "*Juno?*"

But the outwardly innocuous suggestion, which was actually meant to be a joking comparison between Sydney and the titular pregnant teenager in that film, made Sydney's stomach drop with a harsh jolt toward reality. She shot Winnie an *Are you freaking kidding me right now?* look.

"Okay, sorry! You're not like Juno. Totally different scenario. Forget about it. Pick one of the three really dumb chick-flicks on the bottom and maybe it'll put us both back to sleep."

Sydney complied but knew that was never going to happen. She then, predictably, spent the next one point eight hours obsessing and pretending even to herself that she wasn't.

———

While Sydney was thus occupying herself, I was on a rather desperate search for counsel myself. I'd have given practically anything (soul excluded, of course) to have my dear mum with me again, for reasons apart from the obvious love/missing/grieving aspect. I just very much needed to talk the Sydney matter out, have someone give me some cold hard truth, maybe even to successfully reason the notion that I loved her right out of me.

I was thinking these dreary and nearly desperate thoughts that Saturday morning as I sat up early by myself eating cold cereal. Despite having adjusted to the time change by now, I could not yet bring myself to a late sleep-in as the rest of the household seemed accustomed to. I'd risen near the same time every day of my life, and it seemed that neither a different time zone nor a world of exhausting and life-changing grief was about to change that. On weekdays, I wasn't really alone in my arising, as Pam needed to get to school, Uncle Sal to work, and Aunt Jem to . . . housework? Errands? She was a homemaker, it seemed, but I wasn't too sure what else she did with her time. They apparently had exorbitant amounts of money, so there was no real necessity for her to work, but I couldn't help wonder if she were bored with life and if that perhaps accounted for some of her sadness. Or of course, the sadness could be purely from her family members dropping like flies around her.

Just then, I was startled to see her enter the kitchen, already dressed for the day.

And she seemed equally startled to see me. "Calvin! Are you always up this early on the weekend?"

"Typically," I replied. And as she began to go about making her breakfast, I made a quick decision to dive in and have a conversation. Perhaps she could help me with the advice I thought I needed, and in the process maybe I could brighten her day a bit. "Where are you off too?"

"Oh I've a walk-a-thon this weekend. One of those cancer charities. Has a bit more punch to it, this year, considering …"

I wasn't sure how to respond, but she seemed as far away from hysterical sobs at a near-mention of mum as I had ever seen her, so I thought it might indeed finally be suitable to ask. "Can we talk about my mum? Unless you're in a rush."

A pause, but only a brief one. And a small smile. "Guess maybe I can finally speak of her without dissolving to bits about it, hmm? What did you want to talk about?"

I shrugged. "I just feel I have rather a lot of pieces missing still, about her childhood and growing up and things, even though she did tell me more in those last couple weeks than she had her whole life."

She raised an eyebrow. "Missing pieces? Like your father?" Shrewd woman. I nodded. She sighed, sat down with her breakfast. "Well, I probably don't have a lot I can tell you about him, but she met him near the end of our secondary school while he was studying abroad from … UCLA, I think. He took her to a dance, she was infatuated, and …"

"And here I am?" She nodded and took a bite of her food. I had a feeling that was about all there was in her store of info about him. I tried, "Don't suppose you might know anything about him or his whereabouts these days?"

"No, love. I'm sure you have hopes, but …"

"Don't worry, I know about how he didn't want me and all that. But I figure, seventeen years rather changed your tune about my existence, right?" She suddenly looked very uncomfortable. "Insensitive? Sorry. I don't hold a grudge or anything."

She waved this away. "No, it's just that … well you must know how guilty I've felt all these years. And not just because I told her to do away with you. I was bloody pissed and upset, so I went and found my own exchange student. And, well Josh was your age, you know, two months younger. But things obviously turned out wildly better for me than they did for her."

Now I had to know the details, if she was willing to tell them. "How so? Didn't Gram and Gramps kick you out too then?"

"Well, they were raging angry as all hell at their second of two daughters disgracing them. Did give me the boot as well. Difference was that Sal and his daddy's money took me in. He graduated, entered the family business, and we got married when Josh was two and Pam was on the way. And in all that, I never picked up the phone, never did more than look her and you up online. Because I had been so very angry with her, for choosing you over me essentially. And then that anger turned to shame and guilt … And here I am, in therapy two times a week. Lucky me, right?" She gave a little smile with it, as if her heart weren't breaking at the words.

"I had no idea," I floundered, more at a loss as to how to respond when I considered that even her marriage to Sal didn't seem to be much of a happier, better-case scenario.

She brushed my floundering aside. "All this to say, I've had some retribution coming my way for some time, as far as I can tell. And I'd say taking you in—which is not a punishment at all by the way, but more of a consolation—doesn't even begin to cover my debt."

"Well that's no good a way to see it . . ." I tried. I wanted to tell her that God probably wasn't out to give her a lifetime of punishment over her past failings, and to just go confess it all and be done with it, but it's a delicate balance, preaching the Gospel without preaching down someone's throat. So what came out was, "From my point of view, your getting the better end of the deal back then really just set you up for a destiny of being able to take me in and save my precious arse from living on the street." She laughed a little. I concluded, "So thank you, for making use of the gifts God did give you to take care of your splendidly handsome but annoying nephew."

And she laughed wholeheartedly, gave me a little hug.

It was nice. So of course, I didn't have the heart to ruin it by dumping any of my problems upon her.

But Thomas Tucker from California, where I quickly discovered UCLA to be located, he was another story. To my way of thinking, this Thomas Tucker had seventeen years' worth of my problems that were due for his shoulders.

I sat at Josh's desk, the list of numbers narrowed to twelve who lived in California. And I started dialing, fingers nearly twitching with anticipation.

The first was a no. As was the second. And down the line for the next several. I became more disheartened with each try. Until finally, there was a mere one phone number left on the list. I stared at it, wanting to feel in my heart that it was him. But I didn't. I couldn't know. And I was afraid. If I made that call, and it wasn't him either, there was nothing left.

I got an idea and changed course a bit. What if he didn't still live in California? There was no saying he'd ever lived there to begin with, just because he went to school there. So I rolled up my sleeves and tried the thirty-odd non-California numbers I had left. A rather long process, to be sure, and I was met with several voicemail boxes in addition to those numerous confused or annoyed persons I spoke with. So finally, I called it quits, hoping for a positive return to one of those voicemails.

I still had that one last California number, though. It was more likely to be him than any other at this point. And though it felt a bit cowardly, I couldn't bring myself to call him. I feared it wouldn't be him, but I also feared something else that I didn't want to admit: that although Aunt Jem had changed her attitude toward my existence, it really was quite possible that this guy's heart hadn't changed one bit and he still wanted nothing to do with me, perhaps even wished me dead.

With a sigh, I closed the computer and determined to head back distraction-ward. I grabbed my sign and my rosary, and I hopped on my bike, even still embarrassingly oblivious to what I was in for that day.

14

WHILE I WAS EN ROUTE to that certain women's clinic whose sidewalk I'd been frequenting, so was Sydney, but for a completely opposite reason.

Winnie was letting Sydney use her car. Secretly, Sydney had been hoping that Winnie would drive her there and wait for her in the waiting room. But Winnie, as accommodating and supportive a friend as she was attempting to be, didn't even think of that. To her mind, there was no reason she should waste away a whole Saturday morning and early afternoon waiting around, when she could just take a bus and come drive her car back with Sydney in it once the procedure and any recovery time was all over with. Simple enough to Winnie.

But for Sydney, this meant even more time alone with her own thoughts. The drive from Winnie's house to the clinic was about eleven minutes with traffic lights. But it felt like approximately six hours to Sydney. By the third stoplight in, she was so near a total freak-out that she actually grabbed her phone to try to write in her notes app. But it turned out that all those people saying, "Don't text and drive," knew what they were talking about, as she realized, *This is hard!* Changing metaphorical gears, she tried to figure out a voice-to-text note so she could write without typing. And at long last, she figured it out . . . But it felt awkward to say aloud the words she would have written. She tried anyway. "This isn't real. Everything is normal. This isn't real." She tried her hardest to focus on those words, to picture what normalcy would look like in her life.

But by the time she reached the clinic parking lot, she was on the edge of losing it, she was trying so hard to convince herself that the alternate reality was real.

From my vantage point on the sidewalk as I stood there alone before the rest of the group's arrival, all I saw was a car that I thought I recognized without knowing why. The car approached, slowing, turning into the parking lot.

And I saw her. My sad, troubled, future wife. Driving into an abortion clinic parking lot.

The events of the past day washed back over me like a flood of vomit and I realized how stupid I had been to miss this. I felt a rush of the most terrible kind of adrenaline as I came to understand just what was at stake here, and how closely I had come to entirely missing a chance to save her from . . . this.

I walked to the edge of the sidewalk, careful to stay off the clinic property. She got out of the car. Looked up. Saw me. Stopped in her tracks.

I was obviously the last thing she expected to see there, and certainly one of the few occurrences possible to make her mental state even more unstable.

She closed her eyes a brief moment and started murmuring

what was becoming a mantra of sorts, "My life is perfectly normal. None of this is real. This isn't real." And she willed herself to put one foot in front of the other, looking anywhere but at me.

She hadn't even reached the sidewalk when I pounced, willing my tone and demeanor to be casual and not reek of pouncing. "Sydney. Could we have a chat? Say, five minutes? I mean, I'd love a longer chat myself, but I'd settle for five."

She slipped right past me, valiantly ignoring my words and my existence. And I heard her mutter, "Not real. Not real."

I had no idea why she'd be muttering that, but I latched on anyway. "What's that? Who's not real? I sure am. Want to pinch me and see? Just not on the bum, we barely know each other after all." I knew I was starting to flounder, and knowing it only made my franticness increase. And she was nearly to the end of the sidewalk.

Onto clinic property she went.

I took a last desperate stab. "Sydney, please. I know you don't like me much, but you wouldn't wish me dead, would you?"

She stopped in her tracks, turned and stared at me.

"My mum," I explained. "She almost did this, you know? Single, poor, seventeen, her mum kicked her out. Literally everyone and their mum that she gave a damn about in life was telling her to do it. But here I am. She gave me a go."

I couldn't have known it, but Sydney was still hung up on the, "You wouldn't wish me dead, would you?" line. Because she had essentially wished Josh dead, and he was now dead. And then of course she'd also tried to transfer his actions to me . . . Fact and fiction, reality and twisted, pained fantasy were all fighting for her attention and understanding. All that she could get out was, "What are you—just *stop*!" This just as my pal Tatiana came out, most likely to see in what way I was harassing her customers. If I had had my wits more fully about me, rather than scattered in the wind of desperation, I might have noticed how odd it was that Tatiana wasn't immediately interrupting us. That was because she was busy with another task. As I was soon to discover.

Sydney wasn't done spouting her half-formed confusions. If she could have had it any other way, it would have been someone other than me, the object of her imagined loathing and denied attraction, that she was spouting them to; but that couldn't be helped just then. She needed to say them out loud, even though she wouldn't admit to herself that it mattered what I might think. "You don't understand any of this. I don't break rules. I'm one of the *good* girls. I do what I'm supposed to. And *still*..."

I could recognize a poor justification attempt when I heard one. But I could certainly appreciate why the terribly terrible situation she faced was making her try. So all I said was, "Sydney, I know."

"You *don't* know!" she nearly shouted. "I'm about to become a freak again. A raped, pregnant, teenage freak! And it will literally never end, unless—I just can't go back to that after being normal for the past—"

I jumped on her pause, because I knew exactly how long it had been since my arrival here and the coinciding shit-storm that had gone down in her life. And I knew my pregnancy facts by now. "Four weeks? Do you know that your body took two of those weeks for the fertilized embryo—"

She was having none of that. "Just stop it! It's not real! None of this is real! It can't be!"

Tatiana now took the opportunity to swoop in and save

Sydney from big bad old me. She gently took Sydney by the arm, which seemed to startled Sydney. "It's okay," Tatiana reassured her. "I'm here to protect you from him." Now Sydney's brow furrowed. Because she knew, deep down, that there was no need to be protected from me.

But she wasn't getting there, wasn't thinking and acting quick enough. She was letting Tatiana lead her inside. I had to stop it.

"Not real? You think you're dreaming or something? Sorry, but no, it's real. So real that when I do *this*, I'll get arrested!"

And I put my foot over the property line.

Sydney turned back to stare, confused. And Tatiana had absolutely had it. "Get back off the property line! And shut the hell up! Unless you wanna go in for trespassing *and* harassment."

I didn't move, but I had no idea what my next move was, as Sydney and I continued staring at one another. And then, I didn't have to decide my next move, because Tatiana had done it for me, in the moments she'd stood there initially watching us.

Sirens.

"What, you bloody called them before I did anything?"

"I could see where this was headed," she said before turning back to Sydney. "Let's get you inside, hon."

But Sydney was staring at the approaching cop car, confused and even more panicky because of that confusion. She felt foggy in the head. Probably at least a bit in part due to insomnia and pregnancy hormones, but neither of those factors registered on her radar. She was too intently trying to piece together what she had done.

She shook her head. "But … damn it, he's not the one …" She closed her eyes again, and went back to a muttered, "It's not real …"

"Sydney, it *is*," I told her gently.

"Can it, lover-boy!" from Tatiana to me, and to Sydney, "Let's get you inside."

Here, Sydney pulled away from the woman. Looked between me and the cop car, which was now parking quite near us at the curb. She shook her head. And before I knew what she was doing, she was running away, around the corner, back to her car.

Tatiana crossed her arms, sighing angrily. "Wow, I hope you're real proud. One more woman lost to your misogynistic bullshit."

I barely heard her. I was too busy basking in the small victory that was Sydney scurrying off away from this place. And I saw her speed out of the parking lot before the cop even got to cuffing me.

As her car left my sight, I finally registered that my good old friend Frownie Cop was doing the honors and saying, "Wow, this is the guy? Shocking."

I smiled. "Oh hi there, chum. It's down to the station, then?"

And as he started to escort me to his patrol car, I saw Dorothy and a couple others from her group walking over from their cars. I gave her a friendly wave, hoping to ease the horrified look off her face, even as I wrestled with worries over whether they might think something terrible of me.

But I needn't have worried, for Dorothy marched right up to the smug Tatiana and demanded, "Just what is going on here with that nice young man?" And it might seem silly, but it felt kind of refreshing at this point to hear that there was someone left on the earth who thought me so. This thought as Tatiana began to quite thoroughly fill her in on my so-called transgressions, while Frownie Cop shut the door and started to haul me away to a brief incarceration.

———

Thus I began my first ever stay in the big house, as a true American might say. I didn't know that it wouldn't be my last. But as the barred door slammed shut in my face, I felt rather ecstatic. I had just truly helped the girl of my dreams, after all. Certainly I hadn't solved things for her, but at least I'd gotten in the way, quite literally, of her making a further-muddling mistake.

I didn't have long to sit there reveling in my mini victory before Aunt Jem came to collect me. And unfortunately, I was brought quickly back down by the sight of her face.

With a look that I feared might be near tears once again, she came instantly to hug me, the moment they opened my cell. "Oh Calvin, what are you thinking?" she asked into my shoulder. I was taken aback. Given her confession of past regret and guilt to me, I had rather assumed she would understand what I had been thinking. She continued, "I mean, I guess I understand why you might want to be involved in something like that, but please . . ." She pulled back and faced me to look me square in the eye, "Sal will not put up with very much of this, I'm afraid."

Oh. I hadn't even gotten around to thinking of him or his reaction yet. I needed specifics. "What do you mean?"

"He muttered something about kicking you straight out as I was dashing out the door. And dearie, that would just . . ." She hugged me again, and I gathered what it would just.

I could practically feel more stress pile on me, for I certainly didn't want to be the cause of one more break in this poor woman's heart.

15

SYDNEY AND WINNIE'S vague post-procedure plan had involved Sydney calling Winnie when she wanted Winnie to come drive her back, assuming Sydney wasn't able or supposed to drive herself, as they were guessing. Between the fact that Winnie had been the one to make the appointment and perhaps some lack of sound instruction on the part of the clinic in the first place, neither of them was too clear on the specifics of all this. So this calling plan seemed soundest.

When Winnie happened to peak out her window late that afternoon, having not even realized that it was well past the time that Sydney should have called her, she was shocked to see that her car was in the driveway. If Sydney had been okay to drive after the procedure, Winnie had assumed Sydney would have at least given her a call or come inside to let her know it had all gone okay. But not terribly concerned, Winnie just dialed her up.

There was no answer. So with a shrug, Winnie went on

about her day, whose activities included half-assing some homework assignments and primping for a party that evening.

Now, Sydney had in fact not answered for a good reason, that reason being that she was all-consumed with the task of rereading everything she had written in the past four weeks and trying to make sense of what was apparently her real life.

By early evening, she had read it all but was no nearer to being sure she was in touch with actual reality. So she started making piles of the various scenes she had written, trying to separate out what she knew to be true from what she knew to be false. And she soon discovered that there was a lot of material in between. But her mother calling her down for dinner interrupted her from diving too deeply into sorting through that material.

Food was the last thing Sydney wanted to contemplate just then. And she was tempted to tell another half-truth about being sick in order to get out of the meal. But she couldn't. She was already keeping so much from them that at times she started to wonder if it was adding to her generally sickened feeling. While it was true that she had never exactly had a dream relationship with either of her parents, she had certainly never been the type to purposefully lie to them for any reason. In fact, the half-truths she had told them in the past five weeks since she first started dating Josh probably accounted for about 99.4 percent of the parental deceptions of her entire life, that other .6 percent being mostly from around age five when she'd spent weeks at a time acting strangely because she was secretly pretending she was the star of a Disney princess musical.

All that in consideration, Sydney decided it would be best to avoid any further half-truths—pregnancy was a big enough secret, after all—so she went downstairs. And she ate in silence while her mother talked incessantly and poked and prodded into completely inconsequential areas of Sydney's life, and while her father sat there quietly, almost certainly thinking about some kind of nuclear physics issue.

She escaped as quickly as she could back up to her room.

By about eight p.m., she had made a kind of progress in that she had sorted everything into four separate piles: *Pure Fiction, Half True, I Made Happen?* and for the utterly confusing, *Am I on Drugs or Something?*

She was holding on to one last cringe-worthy sheet of paper, whose contents were the events of the afternoon, in which I was arrested. Hesitantly, she placed it into the *I Made Happen?* pile, right on top of a sheet of paper containing the scene of Josh's fiery-crash death. She knew it defied logic, thinking she had actually caused these things to occur, but the facts remained that she had fantasized about very similar events prior to their occurrence.

All that sorting done, she still lacked the clarity she needed, the clarity she'd hoped she would find. She wanted to scream, bash something to bits, but she knew such things would be pointless. Instead, she stared at her phone sitting beside her papers. She was aware that Winnie had called her hours ago, and she finally decided that there was nothing left to do but attempt to talk this out with someone. Winnie, of course, was the only one really available for this task, so Sydney went ahead and rang her, hoping Winnie's brain power and recently waning sympathy would be up for it.

Winnie, by this point, was fully enjoying that party she'd been looking forward to. But to her credit, when her phone rang with Sydney's name, she immediately disengaged herself from the guy she was flirting with, to answer.

"Syd! What the hell? You should have called me or come got me when you brought the car back."

Sydney merely said, "I think I made Calvin get arrested."

Winnie was hoping that she'd misheard this bizarre piece of news under the party noise. "Hold on, I can't hear you." And she stepped aside, farther away from the music. Not observing in the least that a certain person was now standing quite near her. "What now? Did everything go okay?"

In a rush, Sydney recounted an abbreviated version of the afternoon's events, so rushed and abbreviated that Winnie could barely keep up. "Wait, wait, okay hold on. So you're still pregnant?"

I should let you in on just who was listening to this, unseen by Winnie: Kendall. And upon hearing these words, Kendall's gossip-alert senses were one hundred percent engaged, and she immediately turned her attention away from the boring hot guy she'd been all over, in order to listen to Winnie's phone conversation more fully.

"Sydney, get a grip," Winnie was saying obliviously. "Let's focus on the real problem here, the fact that you're ..." And this was where Winnie suddenly felt the ears and eyes on her, turned, and saw Kendall. Gulp. "Uhhhhh, that you're— that you're just too damn smart. And cool. And awesome. Sorry I've gotta go."

And that was it. Sydney stared at her phone in confusion. And with a defeated sigh, she dropped her head onto her desk, trying her best to find hope in the incorrect idea that at any rate, things probably couldn't get worse for her.

I had similarly zero idea that things had taken this increasingly terrible turn. So when I arrived at school on Monday to an unusually abuzz pre-class crowd, I never thought the reason would have anything to do with me or with Sydney.

Rather, I was just pondering how best to scope her out and find a nonthreatening way to approach her. Because I felt I really needed to suggest she get professional help for all this. And, considering that I'd recently won the victory of convincing Pam to at least give counseling a go, I was optimistic about this idea. So I was in the middle of thinking about how this would go down when a random guy I'd spoken to probably a few times in the past approached me, looking conspiratorial.

"Did you hear?" he asked me. I stared back blankly. "About Sydney? She's pregnant! Crazy, right?" I barely had a chance to respond, which was probably better for all involved, before the guy went off on his way, most likely to keep spreading the story around.

And I felt my face settle into a scowl. Oh this would not do. I felt the need to do something drastic about it immediately, but before I could piece together the fact that there was pretty much nothing available for me to pounce upon, Kendall came along and pounced upon me. Not literally, but practically: "Calvin! Oh. My. Gosh. Did you hear?"

Oh goodness. I was going to do or say something in anger that I would very much regret momentarily if I did not get away. So I started walking quickly toward my classroom, completely ignoring this girl.

She did not take the hint but kept pace beside me, chattering on. "I mean, no wonder Sydney was so broken up over Josh. Because *obviously* he was her first, right?"

I could feel the scowl deepen on my face, but I heroically kept my mouth shut.

She giggled. "Don't worry, you've still got me. No pregnancy here!"

"Excuse me," I said, abruptly breaking off toward the men's room so she could not follow.

I didn't know that behind me, Kendall was narrowing her eyes, thinking deeply (which was probably rather difficult for her to do) about how hard to get I was playing, and how it was definitely time for her to pull out all the stops when it came to getting the attention of this (cursedly) dashing British fellow.

—

Meanwhile, Sydney was also hiding in a restroom, because she had figured out pretty quickly what all the gossip was through the halls. And feeling that her normal method of writing and rewriting was rather failing her lately for various confusing reasons, she hadn't the foggiest notion how to handle all this, other than to spend the duration of her school day in a toilet stall. A prospect that seemed as good as any, until she heard, from another stall, "I know, it's so scandalous! Do you think they expel people for getting pregnant?"

A voice from the next stall replied, "Well, and didn't she only have like a couple dates with him? I mean holy crap!"

The first stall, now emerged for hand washing: "Right? I mean, sure, it's Josh, but way to put out!"

And it was just then that Winnie came in pursuit of her

friend, inadvertently making things worse. "Syd? Are you okay?"

The two girls, now both in the outer area, glanced back toward the one closed stall door, realizing their little blunder. With a giggled, "Oops!" they both slipped back into the hall, leaving Sydney to die of mortification in peace.

She came out of the stall to face Winnie, who said, "I'm so sorry, Sydney."

The way in which Winnie said this made Sydney look sharply at her. Slowly, she said to Winnie, "You mean, you're sorry like, 'Why is this crap happening to my friend?'"

Winnie paused just a beat too long before replying, "Right, yeah. That."

"Not sorry like you ... like you told someone or something?"

"I mean ..." Winnie tried to stall, but finally thought what the hell and continued, "I *was* at a party when you called the other night. I guess it's possible, with how close Kendall was standing to me?"

"Kendall? You *told Kendall?*"

"I didn't *tell* her!"

"You might as well have!"

And Sydney stormed past her, not listening as Winnie tried to tell her, "Lighten up! It was an accident!"

⁓

All things considered, it really wasn't much of a stretch for Sydney to claim sickness and head home. I might have been tempted to do so myself, I was so fed up with the whole situation, except that the thought of locating her and offering what assistance I could kept me from throwing in what was starting to feel like an impossible towel.

But while I was contemplating my next possible move, she was at home finally giving in to her desire to play out how sick she truly felt in front of her parents. And of course it was proving to be a terrible idea.

Because she was curled up in the living room with a book that evening, Robert reading one of his smarty-pants journals nearby, while Maryanne somehow managed to hover and smother from the kitchen. And first it was, "Sydney, do you want some soup?"

She replied, "No thanks," and hoped it would stop there, but suspected it wouldn't.

Sure enough: "You know you need to keep those fluids up. This bug sounds nasty. Maybe some juice? An ice pop?"

And Sydney looked up to find her mother already holding both items. "I'm fine, Mom."

Maryanne somehow managed to check Sydney's forehead whilst holding said items. "You don't really feel feverish …"

"It's more just my stomach."

"Nausea or pain?"

Too much. And it was clearly not going to end. Sydney sat up abruptly. "You know, I'm actually starting to feel better. I think I'll get my homework and sit in the yard."

As Sydney then got herself situated in her little yard nest, I once again set out on a course to muddle things up for her.

Through no fault of my own, I had learned where she lived. And just then, as I all but exploded with anxiety for the state of her mind, her soul, and of course her baby, it seemed providential. Considering the veritable storm of misfortune she'd just faced at school, I could hardly see how my sincerely friendly face would still give her a fright. So, with a hope and a prayer that I wasn't about to do something abysmally stupid, I set out on my bicycle toward her home.

I saw her there amid her books in the grass from some distance away, unconsciously cute with her furrowed brow and intense look of concentration. And I inexplicably fell in love all over again. But I shook away the mushy feelings and powered forward, on a mission.

She didn't seem to see me, but there was no other way than the potentially startling, "Sydney?"

She jumped slightly, saw me, and shrank back as I got off my bike and approached, so I decided to stop several feet short of her. "Hey, I'm quite sorry about …" I motioned my head in the general direction of school. "Are you doing okay?" Her response was a joyless laugh. "Sorry, dumb question."

There were a lot of things going on just at this moment that I wasn't aware of. One was that my very presence was only adding to Sydney's general feeling of spent-ness. But the other more significant set of things was that behind her, out of my sight-line, her parents had spotted me, had remembered the creepy things that Winnie had said about me, and even remembered my apparent staring after the play. They were stealthily cracking a window to listen, as Sydney was saying, "So what do you want?"

I replied, "I just want to help you. I mean, the whole thing … It's hard enough that you're pregnant—"

"*WHAT!*"

It was Sydney's father's outraged voice shouting from the house. Sydney jumped up while I instinctively took a step back, looking frantically for the source of the voice.

I didn't have to look long. Robert was out in a matter of milliseconds, seventeen years of self-repressed fatherly behavior forgotten, and trailed by a pale Maryanne.

"You get the hell off my property right now!" he all but screamed at me. I backed up quickly to the street, but I found myself glancing desperately at Sydney, assuming she'd clear the matter up.

And, one look at her panicked face told me she was rather too flustered to think to do so very clearly. All she could get out was, "Dad . . ."

I tried, "It's not what it—"

"Go!" he yelled, and I immediately complied.

There was nothing left for me to do but peddle away and leave them to it.

Sydney had a moment of staring in dumb, confused guilt at her parents, before she started compulsively gathering up her books. It was the only thing that made sense as a course of action: flee from reality once again. For she could hardly begin the task of filling them in on everything taking place in her life, when she was not quite able to put her finger on which elements were real herself.

Maryanne tried, "Sydney?"

"You don't understand. It's not what you're thinking."

Robert asked, "Well are you pregnant?"

She closed her eyes, breathing heavy. Way too real again. She didn't want to talk about it, didn't want to answer their questions and make it even more real. So what came out was, "I'm not—I don't . . ." She was really just trying to convince herself as she muttered, "I'm not pregnant, I'm not pregnant!"

Maryanne tried gently, "What? You're not pregnant?"

And Robert simply had to know. "Just tell us what's going on!"

Before she even thought it through, Sydney blurted out, "I was raped!"

Her parents froze in horrified shock. "Oh honey!" from her mother. And Maryanne immediately tried to wrap her in a hug. Which Sydney very much did not want. All she wanted was to get away from this conversation, so she dashed toward the house.

Robert called after her frantically, "By whom? That boy talking to you?"

She barely paused to offer the insufficient reply, "No! I can't talk about it!"

And she was out of their sight, leaving the two of them to stare at one another, and to decipher whether they were capable of facing this together as a couple or would dissolve to bits in the face of something so truly horrific.

16

NEEDLESS TO SAY, all parties involved in that scene had supreme difficulty sleeping that night.

Sydney's parents, after trying unsuccessfully to coax or pry her out of her room for a conversation, took to a deep discussion between the two of them, the likes of which they actually hadn't had in years. Maryanne was all for calling the cops immediately, but Robert was back to his insanely levelheaded self by now and could see clearly that this was no good until they had some kind of evidence, i.e., a victim able and willing to accuse. Right now, that was not Sydney, so there was no point in going to the law. Just what was to be done, he had no clue. But they discussed and debated for some time, trying to find the best course of action. Though they came up with nothing concrete just yet, they were at least able to firmly take steps toward that coming together option, rather than dissolving to bits. And despite not knowing what they were to do with their currently troubled daughter, they were ready to try and figure it out together.

As for me, I spent the evening and night trying my hardest to decide whether her parents knowing was a good thing. I was inclined to think it was, but I couldn't help feeling terrible for accidentally spilling it to them in such a manner. I wished again, for the umpteenth time, that I had someone to advise me in this unpleasant business, but I didn't dare try Aunt Jem again, for fear of spilling to her Josh's terrible part in it. It was quite possible that she should know, but I remained unconvinced that I should be the one to tell her and didn't relish another accident like I'd caused earlier.

I did once again contemplate calling the last of the Thomas Tuckers. I may have even stared at my phone and at that final number for a few minutes. But in the end, I couldn't do it. I couldn't risk that it would amount to nothing, or worse, and that I would thus lose the small hope I had of finding my long-lost father here.

In the late evening hours, I ended up knocking on Pam's door once again and spilling my guts to her, as the only person who did know of the whole business and all its unpleasant details. She mockingly suggested *I* try counseling, but her lack of practical quick advice did nothing to diminish the relief of talking it out with someone.

And as for Sydney, she obviously fared worst of all the parties involved that night. Morning found her with bags under her eyes, barely held together.

Her mother tried to (figuratively) jump on her the moment Sydney walked down the stairs, and it took all of Sydney's willpower not to scream at her in response. Instead, she told her mother through gritted teeth, "Please, just give me . . ."

"Give you what?" her mother asked, more than ready to instantly give her anything she might need, and hopefully in return get even some small snippet of further information about what exactly was going on.

"A break! Some time! Just, please . . ." And Sydney hurried out the door to school for fresh tortures.

The first was the new strain in her relationship with Winnie. Sydney walked toward Winnie's house, having left her own house early before Winnie arrived to pick her up. They met halfway, and Sydney jumped into the passenger seat like normal, but she could barely even look at her so-called best friend, let alone keep pace with Winnie's stream of light chatter.

Winnie suspected all was not well between them, but she chattered on determinedly, hoping it would just go away.

Sydney, meanwhile, could hardly stop wondering how she could ever trust Winnie again, after Winnie's lack of observational skills had brought about so much new difficulty for Sydney.

And stepping through the doors into the school building only reinforced this sentiment, as the crowd of students seemed to be collectively whispering about her.

From my vantage point as I watched Sydney from a distance, she looked made of stone. Outwardly, she was handling everything decently, it seemed. But I knew it had to be slowly killing her.

I was watching her and pondering it all deeply, so deeply that I didn't notice the rest of my surroundings, namely Kendall jabbering beside me in a tone of voice that was awkwardly seductive. She was saying something about her parents and her house, but none of it registered until I finally noticed her saying, "Calvin? Are you listening to me?"

I glanced her way, my brain catching up with my ears. "Hmm? Parents gone, you say, and I could come over?" Wait, what? "Oh, um . . ." Might as well lay the awkward cards on the table, "You're propositioning me?"

"What the hell?" she said with a flirting laugh. "You don't have to put it like I'm a hooker or something. I just thought, maybe the two of us could get to know—"

Best put a stop to that straight away. "Erm, sorry, no," I cut in. "I'm very much not interested. Nothing personal. Just, no."

That was where I left her, guessing rightly but not really caring that she was watching me furiously as I walked away.

What I didn't know was that she was watching me continue to watch Sydney and was getting some very sinister ideas on what to do about it.

—

It was a matter of hours before I came to learn of the chain reaction I had set off when I so carelessly pissed off Kendall.

I came out of my third period classroom to find the crowd curiously parting around me, almost as if I were the object of their attention. I thought, briefly, that I heard whispers toward my general direction, but I shook it off, thinking it unlikely.

Moments later, as I stood at my locker, a fellow came up to me and said bizarrely, "Way to go, man."

I looked at him, tried, "What's that now?" But he was already moving on. And as I watched him leave, I realized with a start that the sensation of being watched had not been my imagination at all, for it was most certainly happening right now.

I covertly leaned into my locker, picked at my teeth for any embarrassingly huge stray food particles, checked my nose for any foreign matter there, and found nothing. Had someone put a sign of some sort on my back? It seemed not. Trying to write it off to random weirdness, I closed my locker. And I turned to meet the concerned gaze of that priest who had spoken to me a couple days ago as I'd watched Sydney flee the school. I glanced over my shoulder, thinking he might be looking at someone else, as I certainly didn't know him well. But there was no one near me.

The priest suddenly started weaving his way across the river of students between us until he was right next to me. And he spoke in the lowered voice of one attempting privacy: "You know, Calvin—it's Calvin, right?" I nodded. "My door's always open for confession. You seem like a good kid to me. It's okay if you've made a mistake."

Alarmed, I asked, "Have I?" How in the bloody goodness did he even know who I was, let alone about some mistake I'd made that I myself wasn't aware of but that seemed to warrant a confession? I became increasingly alarmed as he left with, "No need to make an appointment. Just drop in any time."

Bizarre as this was, I did my best to shake it off and carry on with my day. But that proved to be impossible, for with each passing step I took down the hallway, I caught more people staring, whispering. And I began to catch snippets of it: "... Taking advantage of her grief ..." And, "How low can you get ..."

Even more alarmed now, I rounded a corner, surprised to see Sydney before me. She was getting something out of her locker and looking every bit as much like wanting to disappear as I was currently feeling.

The weirdness of being watched was starting to get to me, making me careless. I approached her, giving little thought to whether it was going to freak her out anew, but conscious that the interest of onlookers seemed to be increasing with my every step.

"So," I said to her. "I don't know what I did to make headlines lately, but I must say I'm beginning to understand *your* pain of the past day and a half."

She turned to me, anger and total fed-up-ness on her face, just as the warning bell started ringing and saved us from at least two thirds of our audience in the dispersal toward classes. She dropped her voice but stared at me angrily, holding on for dear life to the one emotion that made perfect sense in her screwed-up world. "So make it stop. Go tell the whole school if you want. Tell them everything! Remind them all that I'm the biggest freak they've ever known."

Utterly bewildered, I asked, "What on earth are you talking about?"

"Freaky smart Sydney is pregnant," she began. "Oh guess what? That new British guy is the father. Wow, she's such a slut, her boyfriend *just died*. Oh wait, British guy just set the record straight. So, what, she was just pretending about Josh? She's crazy? Demented? What is wrong with her?" She slammed her locker and started stalking away.

More than a little bowled over, I took a moment digesting it all before I gave pursuit. "Wait, wait," I said, hurrying to catch up. "First of all, you're not a freak."

"Just stop with the fake chivalry or whatever and save yourself. You're obviously not about to go down with me, so go set the record straight already."

"But, no. That's *your* secret. You can't possibly still think me capable of hurting you, exposing you like that?"

Obviously, she did think me capable of it. For by now, without realizing it, the poor girl had become thoroughly disillusioned on the subject of charming princes or wonderful gentlemen coming to her rescue. The type of romance she had dreamed about since she was a little girl, and which I ironically would have died to be able to give her, was now dead to her. "Why shouldn't you! Just *please* get it over with." And with that, she slipped off into a nearby classroom.

I stared after her, but my shock and confusion were mostly wearing off. And turning to anger. Not at her so much as at the fact that I felt abominably thwarted and screwed at every turn, no matter what I did to try and connect with her, help her, even figure her out.

I resisted the urge to punch a locker and carried on toward my study hall, the whispers following me as I went. And suddenly, I'd had enough. Not of the whispers, but of the feeling of uncertainty and the hope that I wasn't floundering and blundering my way along. Dash it all, I was going to call that last Thomas Tucker. Because, damn it, I needed advice and my father owed me at least that.

I had a sickened feeling in my gut as I stood in the parking lot corner usually inhabited by smokers, phone and scrap of paper in my hand. I glanced around, saw no one to overhear me pour my heart out or, alternatively, be crushed, so I gulped and punched the number in. Before I lost my nerve, I pushed the send button.

It rang three times, and the approximate six seconds those rings took felt like an eternity, as I half-panicked and then full-panicked. But then, he answered.

"Hello?"

I swallowed, steadied my voice. "Yes, is this Thomas Tucker?"

"Yeah. Who's calling?"

"Um, I'm trying to locate a Thomas Tucker who was acquainted with a Jan Wilde in London about eighteen years ago?"

A pause. I knew what it meant, because he wasn't hanging up or telling me I'd called the wrong number. My heart quickened.

"Who's asking?" were his next words.

I barely dared, but I had to. Because I knew I had found him. My father.

"My name is Calvin. Wilde. I'm . . . your son."

He swore.

I felt my stomach drop, but I held on, briefly, to the insane hope that it was a profanity of shock, surprise, maybe even joy. When I knew it wasn't.

His voice became gruffer. "Is this some kind of joke?"

"Nooo," I said slowly. "I am in dead earnest, sir."

Silence. I felt my hopes rise. And rise. Could he be choosing his words of joyousness, apology and regret for the past, relief that I was indeed alive and had found him?

And my hopes were answered with a *click*, ending the phone call.

I stared at the phone. The bastard had hung up on me!

I swelled with indignation, disappointment, fury. And I surprised even myself by having the guts to redial.

It rang and rang. The automated voicemail message began, and I tried to think of the words I needed to say to him. But I came up with nothing. I was too thoroughly furious to even try.

———

Moments later, I found myself in the school's chapel.

I've never fancied myself a saint, but I do try. I've mostly put in a good Catholic effort to follow rules, make use of sacraments, say my prayers, the usual.

But right now, as I stood in that simple little room, alone in the aisle, facing God as He sat there both distant and present at the same time in the little gold box, I was so bloody pissed that I didn't even know what a good Catholic should do. Because all I wanted to do was yell and scream and swear at God for letting things be this rotten. What came out was something like this: "My reputation's in the toilet, the girl I love heading further toward crazy-town by the second and still thinks me a terrible hurtful person, and all I bloody wanted was a little fatherly advice! But he can't even be bothered to know I exist. He's too bloody busy doing nothing! Absolutely nothing! For the woman he impregnated or his freaking flesh-and-blood son. And what the hell am I to do? Because it's just more nothing right now! No matter what I do toward Sydney, nothing helps! Bloody, abominable, *nothing*!"

If I'd been saying it out loud, I would have been screaming it at the top of my lungs. As it was, I merely finished with a cold hard stare at the Tabernacle, daring God to do something, anything.

But of course there was no explosion of help or guidance coming to my rescue. So I shook my head and turned to leave, not even a small bit comforted.

And then a strange thought occurred to me. Just a simple everyday thought, in the ringing of my last words repeating through my head. Nothing. Nothing. I said it aloud, "Nothing …" thinking it through, what this doing nothing might look like. Uncertain, I glanced back toward the front: "I'm not entirely sure I can pull off nothing …"

—

By the end of the school day, I had thoroughly determined a new course of action. Or rather, a course of inaction. And I continued mulling it over to the distant sound of whispers about me, as I left the school building and Pam fell into step beside me.

"So," she said, expectantly.

I sighed, knowing exactly what she was referencing with her one-word greeting. "So," I replied.

"Anything you wanna tell me?" she asked. "Or the whole school?"

I shook my head determinedly and laid it all out for her. "I've decided to sit back and keep my mouth shut. Take a reputational beating, prove a point to her, get her to face reality."

She took a moment, before, "You know that's insane, right?"

"Eh, I've heard crazier things."

"She might just leave you to it and keep it all to herself."

I'd thought of that, and I did know that at this point it was definitely a possibility. Yet, as little as I really knew Sydney, I had picked up enough about her beautiful personality to know how she loved the idea of a romantic story, of a sacrificially loving gesture. And our entire situation made an easily recognizable such gesture impossible. So this would have to do. I would sacrifice myself in a way for her greater good, and I had faith in her own innate goodness and optimism struggling to find its way back out from all this trash. So I said firmly, "She won't."

And Pam left it at that, for now.

—

Meanwhile, Sydney had lived through another school day, the gossip mercifully seeming less harsh now that the student body was busier discussing what a horrible slash super cool guy I was for getting her pregnant.

But ironically, once she got home things were worse for her once again, in the form of her concerned parents.

Having made it this far in defying Maryanne's smothering pressure overtly for the first time in her life, Sydney remained steadfast in her refusal to talk about things, and she once again shut herself into her room, pleading homework and actually trying to do it. But that was proving to be impossible, because apart from the ongoing pain, anxiety, confusion, etc., she now also had her mother knocking on her door about every seven minutes, trying anew each time to get some information or offer some supposed comfort.

Just then, like clockwork, her mother was knocking again, asking from the other side of the door, "Can we talk *now*, honey?" By this point, Sydney was holding her head in her hands, dying for some peace. "Please, sweetie. I just want to help."

Worn down, Sydney finally stood and unlocked her door.

Instantly, Maryanne was rushing inside and trying to hug her, saying, "Talk to me, baby. What are you feeling? What do you need?"

Sydney squirmed out of the hug and went back to her desk chair, still no nearer to wanting a discussion about any of this. So she kept her mouth shut.

Maryanne plowed ahead anyway. "Sydney, I am your mother. I want to help you through this. What can I do for you?"

And Sydney, this girl who had never yelled at her mother in their entire seventeen plus years together, finally couldn't take it anymore. "Just back off!"

The instant it was out of her mouth, Sydney knew she shouldn't have said it, as Maryanne worked poorly to keep her face from crumpling. Sydney did her best not to notice this, and Maryanne quickly shook off her feelings of hurt in favor of more well-meant prying: "How long have you been sitting here all alone with this?"

Sydney tried, "I don't want—"

"*When* did it happen, sweetie?"

"I just—I don't—ugh, April second. There, are you happy? Just please, Mom . . ."

Maryanne was finally starting to get a glimpse of the fact that her questions were at least in part the cause of Sydney's current anguish. And, all else aside, at least Sydney had finally given her *something* to work with. So Maryanne stood. "*Please* come talk to me when you're ready."

Sydney didn't respond as her mom left. She was too busy trying to pull herself back into her rapidly deteriorating cocoon of safe oblivion and pretending.

LITTLE DID SYDNEY know that her parents were attempting to come up with a plan of action on her behalf downstairs.

Robert had just arrived home as Maryanne came down the stairs from that mini-conversation. He looked at her questioningly, and she merely nodded. Though they had not been the closest married couple in the past, these most recent twenty-four hours had amazingly re-cemented their dormant one-flesh-union communication skills.

"*April second,*" was all Maryanne had to say.

Robert mulled this over for a moment, nodded. "I think it's obvious she doesn't want to talk to us about it, so we'll let her be and start focusing on the boy who did this to her, now that we at least have the date."

"... That Calvin?"

"We have to assume so, right?"

Maryanne nodded, began taking out the dishes for dinner.

"That seems like the obvious answer, but why …" She tried to piece together her thoughts. Something felt very off about this conclusion.

"Why is she still talking to him? Denying he did anything? As if she's trying to protect him for some reason?"

She nodded. "Yes. I can't even fathom …"

He broke in, certain on their course of action: "We can't be sure of her motive, but here's what I think we should do. First, we let Sydney spend a few days with your sister."

"Yes! That's perfect. Let me give Lisa a call." She was already grabbing her cell phone.

"Then we take tomorrow off, we dig around a little, find out everything we can about what's going on with this Calvin. And if we're lucky, he'll be behind bars before she's back."

Maryanne nodded, relieved, tears stinging her eyes. He took her into his arms, and the two of them clung together as they hadn't in years before yesterday afternoon.

My course was set. I was firm in it and remained so as I once again walked through the doors of school the next day, this time knowing the assumptions I was about to face. I weathered the continued whispers, eager only for first period literature class to start, because I knew I could count on sharing a classroom with Sydney.

Except this morning, she was not there. I stared at her empty seat as the period start bell rang, and I waited for her to come in uncharacteristically late.

By about twenty minutes into the period, I finally came to the unpleasant realization that, now that I'd decided to go all sacrificial lamb for her, she was going to be absent today and completely miss it.

My hope was that she was actually off recuperating in some fashion. And that hope wasn't too far from the truth, as she was presently driving her mother's car up the freeway en route to her Aunt Lisa's house, a grunge rock song that she normally would have hated blaring from the speakers.

———

With Sydney safely out of the way, her parents got to work.

Their first line of action was to call up the principal of St. Aloysius. He was a caring man, typically accommodating and kindhearted, even if a little dense about the way a Catholic school ought to be run. He had already heard the rumors about Sydney's pregnancy, via guidance counselor and chaplain, and he found the matter disconcerting. Though he had never met Sydney one-on-one, he was most certainly familiar with her academic prowess and was fairly convinced that his school would finally have a prominent or even famous alumnus on their hands in the near future. So when Robert called him and asked for a meeting about Sydney, the principal readily agreed.

He met them nervously about an hour later, afraid that somehow he was going to end up to blame for the ruination of the most promising student in St. Aloysius's history.

He needn't have feared, however. Robert and Maryanne had a very specific, information-gathering agenda for this meeting.

Brushing past formalities, as brilliant people are some-times prone to, Robert dove in and asked the man, "Would it be possible to speak with one of your students?"

The man was a bit confused. "Oh. Possibly. Why—or, whom?"

Maryanne cut in, with more social grace than her husband. "You're probably not aware of any of this, but we're trying to get to the bottom of a situation with our daughter." The principal felt his stress level rising, assuming they were talking only about the pregnancy. But then Maryanne startled him by saying, "She's told us she was sexually assaulted."

"By another student?" the man asked, rather aghast.

"Yes," she replied, "but Sydney refuses to talk about it or tell us who."

Robert cut in, "We'd like to speak with Kendall James."

This quite took the principal off guard again. Maryanne quickly clarified. "She and Sydney used to be friends in early grade school, and I now work with Kendall's father. Some things I've heard from him in the past lead us to think she might have information about the situation."

"Ah, I see," the principal said, picking up the phone. "I never did have the impression that she and your daughter were friends, but I certainly believe in Kendall's capacity for, um, well, news and rumors. So you might be right. Let me get her in here for you."

⁓

As they were thus employed, Sydney was pulling into the driveway of a small house in a rather affluent Seattle neighborhood. Her aunt's house.

She barely had time to cut the engine and take a steeling breath before Lisa burst out of the house to greet her. Sydney wasn't sure whether to feel excitement or dread, but considering that her mother had most certainly told Lisa all the details of the reason behind this visit, dread won out.

Nonetheless, Sydney did her best to paste a normal-ish

look on her face as she got out of the car to the sound of, "Hey girlie! Come here!" And a big hug. But not too big, as if something were wrong.

Aunt Lisa grabbed Sydney's bag from her and led her toward the house, singing, "We're playing hooky! We're playing hooky!" It made Sydney crack a smile, despite herself. And amazingly, excitement broke into a small lead over dread.

In the principal's office, Robert and Maryanne had indeed hit a gold mine of apparent information in Kendall.

She was saying, "Oh my gosh, yes! I know *exactly* what's been going on. That Calvin guy has been *all over her.* But wait, back up. Are you saying you think he's like a *predator* or something?"

Maryanne grabbed for Robert's hand, feeling positively sickened despite their apparent good fortune of discovery.

The principal hurried to say, "Kendall, you understand that this remains a strictly confidential matter for the time being?"

"Oh totally, of course!" She made a zipping motion across her mouth.

The three adults, knowing nothing of my complete innocence in the matter, assumed that it would all be in the hands of the police in a matter of minutes anyway, so no worry if this world-class gossip began her inevitable rumor-spreading shortly.

Luckily for Sydney, she was far away from all this and finally relaxing, as she and Aunt Lisa sat with homemade lattes on the couch, discussing books.

All was going splendidly, light and breezy and nontragic in topics, until Aunt Lisa accidentally broached a pain point: "So tell me what you've been working on? I mean since your massive play-writing success?"

Yes, what indeed? Sydney froze, thinking of all the painful and confusing rot she had written in the past four and a half weeks: Josh dying in a car crash, evil-version of me attacking her, escaping the gossip at school, me getting arrested . . .

Sydney tried her best to hold in the flood of emotion that came with the mere thought of all these things. But she was about to lose it. She took deep breaths, closed her eyes, and finally opened them again to find Aunt Lisa staring at her in shocked concern.

"Sydney?"

Sydney couldn't help it, the tears just started flowing, out from beneath her closed eyelids. Aunt Lisa set down her coffee cup and immediately went to hold her, saying, "What is it? Just tell me, and we'll get through it together."

Sydney sputtered, "But—but, we can't! I'm pre—I'm preg . . ."

Lisa gently asked, "You *are* pregnant?" Because Maryanne hadn't been exactly clear on that issue herself when she'd told Lisa the details.

Sydney's response was more tears, but she managed a small, almost imperceptible nod before trying to hide her face and pretend this wasn't happening.

Now this was the kind of thing that really set Lisa off, situations like this. She got antsy, hard, as she pulled back to her own corner of the couch, deep in thought. "So let me see if I've got this right," she began. "You were raped. You tried to move on, forget about it, probably even tried to write it away somehow?" Sydney nodded miserably in response. "But now you have a constant reminder *inside* you?"

Sydney nodded weakly but couldn't look at her. Lisa grabbed Sydney's face and gently but firmly turned it toward her. "Let's make this pregnancy go away. That's the first thing we can do about all this."

"I don't . . . I don't know if I can." In truth, Sydney had been doing her best not to think about the details of the encounter between the two of us that past Saturday, but she was very unconvinced on what she *should* be doing, what she would have done if I hadn't been there. "I just, I think and I think . . ."

Lisa nodded. "You're thinking too much. Just forget about everything else and focus on how you can have a normal life."

Sydney looked back at her, wide-eyed and uncertain. She wanted to believe her aunt's words and look forward to a so-called normal life as a real possibility again. And the lure of such a prospect was such a pull that, despite all her uncertainties, she found herself nodding.

———

Having gotten the information they thought they needed from Kendall, Robert and Maryanne were finishing up with the principal.

There was probably a protocol for all this, steps the principal should be taking with the specifics of the situation that he was now learning, but he was facing two very concerned and rather intimidating parents. So he was basically doing whatever they wanted in order to help them. Which, incidentally, was just grand for my situation.

He was looking up information from my file to give

straight to them. The phone numbers for my current guardians.

"Since Calvin didn't start here at St. Aloysius until after spring break, you should definitely confirm with his aunt and uncle when he arrived in Seattle, if you're at all uncertain that he's the culprit."

"Of course. Thank you very much," Robert was saying as they stood and took the copied number from the man.

And, that completed, the two of them rushed straight out, on a mission. Just as second period ended.

They found themselves in a swarm of students as they made for the front door of the building. And in that swarm, I saw them.

I stopped in my tracks, a confused and sickened feeling in my stomach. Not knowing yet that Sydney had even told her parents she'd been raped, I didn't know exactly what was going on. I had a feeling it was something terrible, but I put my head down and carried on, determined to carry out my plan of silence.

Of course I had no idea that the two of them were rushing to the car to make a phone call to my uncle.

Sal picked up immediately. Maryanne leaned in close to listen as Robert said, "Yes, hello. This is the father of one of your nephew's classmates."

Sal was more than fed up with troublesome me by now. "What, did he do something to your kid, I suppose?"

Robert and Maryanne glanced at one another in sickened certainty that they'd found their culprit. But Robert carried on, "That's actually what we're trying to figure out. We're wondering if he was living with you on April second?"

That fateful day. Sal remembered it well, as the night

that his son died. And also, "Yes, I remember distinctly. He went out running around in his pajamas like a weirdo at ten-thirty p.m."

Bingo. And thus was my fate sealed. Robert and Mary-anne nodded at one another. "Thank you," Robert said on the phone. "That's all we needed to know."

End of phone call. And while the two of them hopped onto the task of getting my arse dragged to jail, Uncle Sal called up my poor aunt in exasperation.

No need to recount more of their marital discord and the end result of Aunt crying over me and my future as a booted-out kid on the street. Much more to our interest is what was occurring at school just then.

I was walking along between classes and wishing I'd brought ear-buds to school, despite typically disliking the practice of nonstop music listening, when Pam trotted up breathlessly.

"Calvin!" she called to me. I was startled by her ruffled demeanor. She came up close before whispering, "Something's wrong."

"Shocking," I quipped, carrying on my way while she walked beside me.

"No, really wrong. You know that Kendall girl? She's talking some serious shit about you."

I shook my head and brushed it off with a joke, no real understanding just yet: "Women. One minute she's throwing herself at me, the next—"

She cut me off. "No, listen! I think you're—maybe I'm wrong, but it sounds like people think you ..."

I looked at her, waiting for her to spit it out. And finally, she croaked, "... Raped Sydney."

I stopped walking, cold dread washing over me. "No."

She went on, though I barely heard her. "So I'm thinking, what have you got? Alibis? Witnesses? I mean, no one knows about Josh but you and me, but like if she's really pregnant they can figure out the date I think and—"

I was quite zoning off from her words by this point, a deep panic creeping upon me. Because, first, I was rumored to be the father. Terrible, sure, when it was so violently opposed to my true character and actions. Now, I was said to be the rapist father. On the day Sydney was absent and unable to see my silence or say a thing or be jolted to the reality of what her pretense was now doing.

And yet, I'd made a decision, in favor of silence, in hope of saving her. I couldn't turn back now, not when I still had even a glimmer of a chance that this could work, could save her.

I snapped back to the reality of Pam speaking to me. And I cut her off: "I just need to know where she is."

"Calvin, I'm saying you can't count on her. She's a head-case."

"Well she's my headcase!" I snapped. "Or, if she isn't, then she will be." I quickened my pace, toward the front of the school, thinking rapidly. "I just need to bloody know where she is, make sure she knows what's going on."

Pam kept pace beside me, nearly dripping with exasperation. I could practically feel her trying to find the words to tell me how stupid I was being, when the sight before us made us both stop cold.

Frownie Cop was walking through the doors of the school, staring straight at me.

18

SYDNEY AND LISA, meanwhile, were having a similarly spectacular time as they set off in attempt to solve Sydney's problems.

Mere minutes after they discussed the issue, Lisa had secured her an appointment at a somewhat higher-class women's clinic than the one at which we had had our encounter. The whole fifteen-minute ride there, Sydney was doing her best not to think about any of it. An absolute failure. By the time they pulled into the parking lot, she was tightly gripping her seat and didn't even realize it. Lisa spied the death grip but didn't comment on it a she turned the car off and opened her door. Sydney slowly opened hers as well, gathering her things like a robot: purse and notebook.

Now Lisa had to comment. "Do yourself a favor and leave the notebook." Sydney hesitated. Dare she leave her lifeline? Lisa told her, "Trust me, there's nothing here to remember. It'll be much easier if you keep your mind totally blank, okay? Don't even think. We'll read magazines."

Sydney glanced back at her notebook with a hint of longing, like a toddler leaving her blankie. But she gritted her teeth, resolved herself, and shut the car door on her beloved writing apparatus.

"There. Okay, we're set," Lisa was saying. "Oh, and cellphones. Might as well turn them off now so we don't forget. They're usually pretty strict on it here." Lisa turned off her own, and Sydney numbly did the same. "It'll be all over with before you know it."

Sydney tried to nod in agreement. But she couldn't. Because she didn't believe it.

—

As for me, I knew the instant I saw him that Frownie Cop was there on my account.

Sure enough, a matter of moments later I was being formally arrested. I didn't resist, as I presume he expected me to. Instead, I stood meekly and let him snap the cuffs on my wrists, said nothing in defense or protest as he announced the charges. He seemed to me to be rather enjoying it all, a bit smug in the face, but really who could blame him at this point in our relationship.

Beside us, Pam looked rather unconcerned to the casual observer, but I knew her well enough by now to know that she was quite dismayed.

And of course, a crowd of my fellow schoolmates was gathering, larger by the moment. They were watching. Staring. Pointing. Outwardly, I remained stone.

But then he started to lead me away to his squad car, and my heart rate quickened. Because it just *couldn't* be for nothing.

I twisted to see Pam. "Call her!" I ordered. "You have her number, right? Hurry! Let me tell her!"

"Now?" she asked in confusion.

Frownie Cop put in, "Oh he's not making any phone calls right now."

I ignored him and yelled to Pam, "Put it on speaker!"

But she was still trying to pull her phone out of her bag, trotting to keep up with us. Frownie Cop only increased our speed to get away from her.

Finally, she got the phone and was hitting the number. I twisted toward her so my voice might be picked up, but she was listening to the phone and shaking her head. "Straight to voicemail."

Frownie Cop had had about enough. "He'll get his damn phone call later. You want to go in too, for obstruction of justice?"

She spat back, "I'm not in your way, you've got nothing on me!"

We were getting too near the squad car. It was now or never. "I'll leave a message. Speaker, Pam!"

She held her phone out and tried her best to get close to me with it as Frownie Cop did *his* best to get between the two of us, push me farther away from her and the phone.

I didn't care. I knew in my gut that it was now or never to lay it all on the line, if I had any hope of escaping a pointless prison sentence. So no one was going to stop me from calling out absurdly my feelings for the woman I loved, for the whole world to hear, almost quite literally: "Sydney? It's Calvin. It seems I'm being arrested, because I believe in you, and you're extraordinary, and I need you to be extraordinary right now, and I don't care if even the whole world thinks you're a freak, because I love you!" This last bit literally as Frownie Cop was shoving me into the back of his squad car. He slammed the door shut with a righteous shake of the head.

And I watched through the window as Pam finished the message with, "And he's gone."

—

Sydney was doing her best to take Lisa's advice and keep her mind blank. Such a simple task, when every which way she looked was something like an STD info-graph, and the very magazines were all about sex or reproductive health. *The Scarlet Letter*'s tendency to remind her of that which she wanted to escape was nothing compared to this crap. The inability to look anywhere without a reminder was seriously affecting her already unhinged mental state, as the minutes ticked by with literally nothing to occupy her mind that wasn't related to her predicament. Her appendages became jittery without her even realizing it until Aunt Lisa gently put a hand on Sydney's bouncing leg.

Lisa was about to say something in attempt to calm and reassure Sydney, but she was saved from this legitimately impossible task by a nurse calling, "Sydney?"

For a brief, terrible moment, Sydney could not move. And then Lisa said, "I'll be here the whole time. You'll be fine."

And Sydney found herself nodding again, latching onto the phrase and repeating it silently to herself: *I'll be fine. I'll be fine. I'll be fine.*

Before she knew it, she had followed the nurse back to a patient room. And moments later, Sydney was undressed, in a gown, clothes folded neatly on the floor. Ready to wait.

More jitters, and nothing substantial to latch onto again. She hopped down from the table and started pacing. There were already instruments of some kind laid out, but she purposefully kept her gaze far, far away from them.

And suddenly, *I'll be fine* wasn't nearly good enough anymore. She needed something stronger. She tried her go to: *This isn't real, this isn't real.* Another no-go.

She went to the counter, rummaged out what looked like it might be a pen … definitely wasn't.

And she couldn't take it anymore. She had to write, there was no other way about it. So she went to her purse and took out her phone, turning it on despite standing literally right under the TURN YOUR FREAKING PHONE OFF! sign.

It felt like an eternity before her phone finished powering up. But then, in blissful relief, she opened up the notes app to start typing.

Until, *chime.* Voicemail.

She shot a quick guilty glance at the door but put the phone to her ear to listen anyway. "Sydney? It's Calvin …"

She listened to my message, her heart rate increasing with each word. She grabbed the counter for support—*I'm being arrested…extraordinary…I love you!* And of course Pam announcing that I was gone.

Reality crashed into Sydney hard. She stared at her phone, tears inexplicably gathering in her eyes. She was confused, or wanted to be. She had to listen to it again, lifted the phone back to her ear.

And the door opened.

The nurse returned, this time with the doctor. The nurse spotted the phone instantly, with Sydney standing poetically beneath the phone-off sign. "Naughty, naughty." And she took the phone gently out of Sydney's hands, turning it off. "Whatever it is, I'm sure it can wait." It's quite possible that a person had never been more wrong. The nurse went on to emptily reassure her with, "This will all be over before you know it."

And in that instant, Sydney knew this wasn't true. Sudden clarity was washing over her, though she was fighting it. The nurse led her to the table, and Sydney obediently hopped up, eyes still on the phone as my message ran through her head, reminding her what was real, what her silence was doing.

The doctor was doing doctorly things with the instruments, in preparation, and the nurse was adjusting Sydney down into the stirrups. The doctor said, "I need you to relax," but her breathing quickened.

She tried her best to dive back to oblivion with a muttered, "This isn't real, my life is normal, this isn't real." It didn't work anymore. Perhaps it never had. She opened her screwed shut eyes to the sight of a very real needle and syringe in the doctor's hand.

The doctor began lifting her gown and said, "I'm going to give you a local anesthetic now."

And in that moment, she couldn't fight reality any longer. She knew.

She knew that none of this messed-up situation would be over, even if she went through with this. It could never be over. There was no going back, no erasing all this, no matter how much she wished, dreamed, or wrote it so. Sydney suddenly saw this with more clarity than she had known anything in her whole life.

She gasped out, "Wait!"

The doctor, startled, pulled back and paused. And she ripped her feet out of the stirrups, sat up, hopped down.

The nurse privately rolled her eyes before putting a calming hand on Sydney's shoulder. "Honey, you're fine."

Sydney now knew this was a lie, and for the first time in the past four and a half weeks, she embraced the truth of the matter. "I'm not."

Before the nurse or doctor quite realized what was happening, Sydney had grabbed her purse and her stack of clothes. And she dashed out the door.

19

SIMPLE AS IT MIGHT BE to turn tail and run away from a scary needle, scarier instruments, and some falsely comforting nurse, the rest of what Sydney now knew she had to do was a bit more complicated. Starting with facing her aunt.

Sydney burst into the waiting room, a strange sight indeed in her gown, and Lisa wasn't the only one staring. "Sydney! What are you doing?" Lisa exclaimed in an indiscreet whisper.

"I need to go! Take me back to your house."

But Lisa's response was a sigh, and not the least bit of the urgency that would come with understanding of just how desperate Sydney really was right now. Instead, Lisa said gently, "Sydney, you're panicking. It's okay."

"No, I'm not!" Sydney said frantically. "I need you to help me, please! I'll explain everything in the car."

Lisa wasn't buying it. She took Sydney firmly by the shoulders. "Sydney, breathe. Relax. Calm down. You can do this. You can take back control of your life if you—"

And Sydney was having none of that, because taking back control of her life was precisely what she was doing by running out of that place. So she spat out, "I am!" And took off at an awkward run, holding her gown closed over her backside and her stack of clothing under her arm.

Once outside, she felt a rush, exhilarated and knowing she was doing what she should have done ages ago.

But the reality was that her gown was making her dash more than clumsy, and she was already winded, probably courtesy of the little one in her womb. The thought gave her a sickened jolt, but now was not the time to ponder it more fully, because she was nearing the bus stop, just as the bus was pulling in.

Still too far off, she sprinted for it, as the doors started to close. Frantically, she waved at the driver, relief washing over her as the doors opened back up for her.

And finally, the poor girl found a seat. Willing herself to ignore the strange stares from strangers, she pulled on her clothes as discreetly as possible under and over her gown. And, settling in for the bus ride to Aunt Lisa's, she prepared to get down to business.

—

While all these earth-shattering things were going down in Sydney's world, I was en route to the big house, for a second and much more significant time. This was no mere trespassing charge, and I could only imagine that Sal and Jem were having it out over my immediate disowning at that very moment. Of course, if it were true, they had every right to disown me. The real question was whether they thought it possible that it could actually be true. This was really not a pleasant thought. Because obviously when I had decided my course of inaction, I didn't realize I'd be briefly allowing the whole world to think me guilty of a fairly terrible crime. That harsh reality was setting in about now, as I thought of how not only my aunt and uncle but teachers, that priest, and heck even that sweet old lady Dorothy, were bound to hear of it. And how could I expect them to not immediately assume something like this was true? Had I made a strong enough impression of my moral character upon everyone whose opinions I somewhat cared about, that they might at least hesitate to make immediate judgment when they heard the rumors?

Of course I couldn't know the answer to this. Right now, I only had to hope that it would be worth it, that Sydney would be jolted into proclaiming it wasn't true, and that all would somehow be kind of well.

It wasn't a perfect plan, I knew that. So many chances, risks, what ifs. I quite understood why Pam was beside herself and calling me an idiot. But I had to try.

A voicemail was risky. I had no idea when or if Sydney would listen. That was my biggest fear, that I was putting myself through this without her having the foggiest clue it was going on.

With a deep breath, I let go of all these fears and re-re-solved myself to carry on with what I felt in my heart was the right course of action. And the patrol car pulled into the police station.

Having been through this once before on the trespassing issue, it was far less intimidating now than it would have been. With a few calming breaths, I found my heart rate steadying, my demeanor back to confidence and casual goodwill as Frownie Cop briskly pulled me to the booking area. I tried to relax and to remind myself that I still had a bit of time for Sydney to show up. Booking, as I'd discovered the last time around, did take a bit. She might even make it here before they were halfway through.

And my hopeful thoughts along these lines were cut short some minutes later by Pam bursting inside. I'd seen her asking another gawking student to give her a ride, so I wasn't surprised to see her arrive. But I was surprised to see her rushing toward me, holding out her phone.

"She's calling! She's calling!" she shouted to me.

"Answer it!" I ordered.

"Sydney?" she said into her phone. "Where the hell are you?"

In truth, Sydney was still on the bus, watching for her stop to get back to Lisa's house. She told Pam, "I'm coming! Don't let them arrest him. He didn't do anything!"

"Well *I* know that, but they're like booking him or something . . ."

I was straining to hear her and then straining harder as I realized I was already being led off toward a cell. "What, you're done with me already?" I asked the booking officer, who merely nodded and pushed me along, farther away from that phone call.

"What's happening? Who's pressing charges?" Sydney was asking frantically.

Pam replied anxiously, "I don't know all the details, something to do with Kendall, and I think maybe your parents? Just get down here as quick as you can!"

And Pam hung up to try to follow to the holding cell, leaving Sydney near panic on the other end.

"Hey, wait—" But it was too late; Sydney realized the call had ended. And that her bus was at her stop.

Almost too late, she hopped up just as the bus started moving again. "Stop, wait!" she called to the driver. "I have to get off here."

The bus driver complied, as she shoved her way to the front. And she flew out the bus doors, sprinting the short distance to Aunt Lisa's house.

She arrived breathlessly at her mother's car parked in the driveway, just as Aunt Lisa's car flew into the driveway. She knew Lisa would try to stop her and probably all but drag her back to the clinic. So Sydney dove into her mother's car, as Lisa hurried out of her own car toward Sydney.

"Sydney, wait! Let me help you."

Sydney had a feeling it would be pointless, but she gave it a quick try anyway before shutting her door to back out: "If you really want to help me, call my parents and tell them—"

Lisa cut her off. "Let's leave your parents out of this. I think we both know they'd have a problem with what you need to do. Just let me drive you back to the clinic, and we'll get through this together."

"No, listen! There's a guy in jail, a good guy, and it's because of me. I have to go!"

She slammed her door shut and put it in gear to back out, fast. Lisa instinctively jumped out of the way, but she called out, "Sydney, this isn't healthy!"

Sydney gave her no second thought and zoomed off.

Willing herself not to analyze, look ahead, or think about anything but the cold hard facts she had determined to be true, Sydney sped back through the Seattle streets toward her house. Or tried to. There's not much speeding on Seattle streets. The feeling of inaction was killing her as she sat behind traffic and paused at stoplights.

She pulled out her phone and tried her parents, though she knew it wouldn't be pleasant.

Robert and Maryanne were actually braving Seattle traffic themselves, en route to come identify me at the police station. Maryanne was startled when her phone rang with a call from Sydney. She forced a smile onto her face to carry into her voice, as she picked up. "Hi sweetie, how's it going?"

By now, Sydney was weaving in and out of traffic, rather frantic. "Mom! What's going on? You guys are wrong about Calvin if you think—"

Maryanne cut her off. "Did Winnie or someone call you, honey?"

"Yeah, and—"

"Sweetie, listen," Maryanne said in her best attempt at a reassuring tone, "I want you to relax at your aunt's, have a good time, and forget about all this. You're safe now. He's behind bars." This just as Robert pulled into the police station. "I have to go now, but I want you to *relax*. Okay? Everything is fine now. Bye bye."

And Maryanne hung up, feeling disturbed and drained. "She's still trying to tell me he didn't do it . . ."

"We're doing the right thing," Robert reassured her. Maryanne nodded, knowing that all signs did indeed point to this being true.

And then, her phone rang again. "Ah, it's Sydney again." She hesitated. "I can't answer this. She'll try to convince me, won't she?"

"Quite likely," Robert concurred.

Maryanne decisively put her phone on silent, though she felt a little rotten doing it. "There. Now I can—I can distance myself from this strange, emotionally charged attachment she seems to have to this guy . . . right?"

Robert nodded. And Maryanne tried to feel right about it.

Sydney, for her part, briefly gave up on her mother after trying a couple more times, and she tried calling her dad instead. But Robert almost always had his phone on silent anyway, because he never really wanted his genius thoughts to be disturbed by the intrusion of someone trying to get a hold of him. Presently, he was occupied with thoughts quite different from his usual genius ones, but he'd certainly not thought to turn his phone ringer back on. So Sydney once again heard endless rings and a voicemail greeting.

We'll leave her retrying these two again and again for lack of better or less frustrating ideas, while Robert and Maryanne went about their unpleasant task.

That unpleasant task being ensuring that I would remain incarcerated.

I knew nothing of what was about to come at me. I was sitting on a small cot in my holding cell, watching the various happenings in the outer area. So many criminals coming and going. And me.

If I'm being honest, I might have expected to be arrested at some point in my life for something small and petty. I'd had some mates earlier on in my teen years who got quite a laugh with me for small things like ringing doorbells and running off, or making graffiti signs. I'd never been terribly into these activities myself, but I had hung around with the chaps as they'd done it. So I'd definitely thought any poten-tial incarceration in my future would be for something along those lines. Certainly not something like a heinous sexual crime accusation.

These were the thoughts occupying me when I was taken completely aback by the sight of Sydney's parents out in the lobby.

I felt my stomach drop once again, as I hopped up. They were coming toward my cell. Of course they were. Quite unlikely they'd have other business here, after all. Okay. No problem. Just have to face the parents of the girl I'm accused of raping. Nothing to worry about, right?

My thoughts raced toward panic level, and I suddenly realized I was praying a wordless prayer that somehow, some way, Sydney would burst through those doors before I had to face them.

But that didn't happen.

An officer was walking them over to my cell. Maryanne stopped several feet short, looking like she might vomit at the refuse (me) she was seeing. I heard her murmur disgustedly to the cop, "That's definitely him."

But Robert kept walking. All the way up to my cell door, until he and I were facing one another. I forced myself to stare innocently back at him. I had nothing to hide, as much as I felt I needed to crawl away and die somewhere. He narrowed his eyes at me, seemed to search down deep inside himself for words vile enough to condemn such a monster (again, me). And apparently, he could find none. Because he spat on me.

And Robert turned and walked away, leaving me staring at the blob of spit on my arm and mulling over what that first family dinner with me at their house might look like after all of this was over.

———

Sydney, meanwhile, had finally given up on trying her parents for the time being and had moved on to Winnie. "Come on, pick up, pick up," Sydney murmured as it rang back in her ear.

Finally, Winnie picked up. "Syd?" she said warily. Winnie wasn't sure how this phone call was going to go. The two of them were already barely on speaking terms since Winnie's careless goof, and now Winnie had this piece of information about me. She had heard of it quickly enough at school, just like the rest of the student body had, but Winnie assumed that Sydney was oblivious to it. And she wasn't sure whether it was a good idea to tell Sydney . . . But she also wasn't sure she could keep this juicy piece of news to herself.

Luckily for Winnie, Sydney quickly solved that dilemma for her: "Winnie! I'm so glad you picked up. Listen, they arrested Calvin. They think *he* raped me, and I'm on my way back from my aunt's—"

Winnie was so relieved about the fact that she didn't have to decide whether or not to tell her, that she completely missed the urgency in Sydney's voice and said, "Oh I'm so glad you already heard! And isn't it like so totally poetic? Since he like tried to attack you or whatever that one time? He totally deserves it. I figured I should tell you so you could like celebrate or something, but I didn't wanna dredge stuff up again about it . . ."

Sydney was dismayed. "No, no! He never did anything! Listen—"

Now Winnie was getting frustrated. "Wait, but you said—"

"I know what I said!" Sydney took a deep breath, trying to keep herself from screaming at her former best friend.

I think they both knew. If they had been growing apart a little bit in the months leading up to all this garbage, the events of the past weeks were driving an elephant-sized wedge between them. And that was a shame. They both thought so. But right now, all that was coming out on either side was a lot of frustration.

Winnie spat out, "Okay, Sydney I don't know what to believe from you anymore. You tell me one thing, then you say it's not real, then you say it's a story you wrote, then you say it's real again. Why can't you just talk to me like a *normal person*?!"

And all hell broke loose inside Sydney. "Because I'm not a normal person! And you've always known that! What I'm telling you now is what's real. And I get that I haven't made it easy for you to understand what's going on, but if I'm being honest, your advice so far has really sucked. So you know what? I don't care what you think anymore. If you don't want to help me, fine. I can and will do this myself."

And she hung up, almost too pissed to cry. Almost.

She wiped her eyes on her sleeve and sped on.

Maryanne didn't think to turn her phone ringer back on until they were pulling into their driveway once again. She pulled her phone out as they parked, and she gasped.

"Robert, I have twenty missed calls from Sydney."

He looked at her sharply, pulled out his own phone to check. Twelve. He went to his voicemail, while Maryanne was already listening to one. "Wait, listen to this," she was saying. "It's from Lisa." He leaned to listen.

"Hey, I'm really worried about Sydney. She just took off. She's been saying things that don't make sense, and it really sounds like she has some sort of attachment to the guy that raped her. I have to wonder if she's having some kind of mental break."

And thus the two of them became even more prejudiced against hearing the true story behind all this. If Maryanne had been wavering, her maternal heart breaking at the thought of disbelieving her only, beloved daughter, her resolve was now hardened. If there was any room for doubt in Robert's clear and logical mind that they were doing what was best for Sydney, it was now banished completely. The two of them knew that they couldn't believe any objections she might offer.

So when Sydney came barreling into the driveway just a few minutes later, they thought they were ready.

She got out and started at a run toward the door. And they were there to meet her. "Sydney, I just talked to Aunt Lisa," her mom said, but Sydney cut her off.

"You guys screwed up. Calvin didn't rape me."

Her mother put an intendedly comforting hand on her arm. "Sweetie, you don't have to pretend anymore."

And before Sydney could react to this, she was shocked to feel her father's hand on her arm. She couldn't remember the last time he'd hugged her. Right now, he was firmly leading her inside, and it was so strange to her that it nearly distracted her. For a moment, before: "No! I'm not pretending anything. Calvin is *good*, and he's trying to help me! We need to go down to the police station and tell them—"

Robert cut in firmly, certain on the best course of action. "Sydney, you're delusional. But it's okay. We're going to take care of you."

He began to pull her a bit more forcefully inside. So she twisted away. "No, listen to me!" And before anyone knew what was happening, Robert was essentially shoving her toward the stairs. Enough so that Maryanne started to feel a little uncomfortable.

"Robert . . ."

But he was adamant. "She's sick. You know she is. We have to help her." Maryanne agreed, but it didn't feel right to shove their daughter up the stairs.

Especially as Sydney continued yelling, "You have to listen to me!"

He put her inside her room, shut the door. She pulled on it frantically from the other side, but he held it shut. "Get me a screwdriver?" he said to his wife. Maryanne anxiously hurried to comply.

She gave it to him, and he quickly unscrewed the door knob, half opened the door, interrupted by, "Let me out!" And he put the knob back on, backward, clicking the lock from the outside.

He and Maryanne both heaved a sigh of relief, looking at each other with concern as Sydney yelled at them, "Calvin didn't rape me! You have to believe me!"

"What if—" Maryanne started to whisper, but Robert cut her off.

"We can't waiver. We know the facts. We have to protect her."

Maryanne nodded, tearing up, feeling that they had failed radically to do a good job of that so far.

"Let's give her time to cool down," Robert suggested. So, drained, the two of them headed back downstairs.

But on the other side of that door, Sydney was hyped-up and determined, as far from cooling down as you could get. She was rummaging in her desk, searching for anything that might serve to get her out of this makeshift prison.

And instead, all she came out with was a stack of papers. Her stories. Taunting her.

Even though she figured her parents had gone downstairs to further discuss how crazy she was, she couldn't help but yell, "It's all fake! I was trying to change it! Please. Look at these! You have to let me out!" But she knew it was pointless.

She sank to the ground, staring at the stack of papers. And suddenly, she got an idea.

Going back to the desk, Sydney ripped open a drawer in search of something specific. More rummaging, until she came back out with … a scented candle. Not quite what she was looking for. She dove back in and located her prey: a box of matches. Bingo.

She pulled her desk chair over to the fire alarm. Struck a match and stared at it. Gulped. Now or never. "Goodbye, old friends. You were screwing up my life anyway." And she held the flame to the corner of her stack of recent stories.

They caught instantly.

Beep, beep! The smoke alarm.

Calmly, she hopped off the chair, still holding the burning papers, and moved toward the door, satisfied as she heard her parents thumping up the stairs.

"Sydney?" Maryanne was saying from the other side, and the lock jiggled open a moment later.

Sydney shoved the burning papers toward her parents and shoved her way past them.

She heard them exclaiming behind her, dropping the papers and stamping them out. Without stopping, she called back to them, "It's all fake! Everything but Josh and—and—just read them!"

Her parents didn't do as instructed, but Maryanne did stop to pick up the smoldering papers before taking off after Sydney with Robert.

Sydney didn't stop though she heard them behind her.

Instead, she sprinted all the way to Maryanne's car, thankful she had left the keys in the ignition. She started the car and peeled out of the driveway, while Robert and Maryanne jumped into Robert's car and gave chase.

Being hopped up on adrenaline, it took Sydney a few moments to realize how ridiculous all this was. She finally tells the whole truth, and *now* no one believes her? It was such irony that she almost had to laugh. In truth, it was the closest she had felt to actual mirth in the weeks since all this began. And strangely, in much the same way as I had amid the pain and absurdity of my first days in the Simpson home, she began to laugh, as a deep relief spread through her, a feeling that everything was going to be all right. While I had, in those early days, found my comfort in the crazy thought of my mother and Jesus laughing at a joke with me, here was Sydney finding her own peace of mind in the realization that her life truly was a story, well planned and coming to a more thrilling resolution than she could have written herself.

And this realization of hers, it didn't solve much, if anything. It didn't turn her life suddenly to roses and candy. It was no explosion of help like she might have wanted back when she made the brief, hopeless prayer for God to fix everything. And yet, it came with a particular peace and certainty, a reassurance that she would come back to and ponder for possibly the rest of her life.

Right now, though, she had much more pressing things on her mind. Things like avoiding her parents' car as she weaved in and out of the Seattle traffic once again, this time on her way to save the guy she now realized was not an opponent at all.

Finally, at long last, Sydney was able to start to see my efforts as those of a guy who cared deeply for her.

20

I, MEANWHILE, had had quite a day of it. It seems that the business of being wrongfully accused, and everything that had followed for me, can really take a toll on a fellow.

I was fighting to keep my spirits up, to remain in hope that I wasn't being an absolute idiot and that Sydney really would come to and step up. Pam remained waiting faithfully in the lobby, doing no good whatsoever out there, other than encouraging me by her non-desertion. But in addition to her, now, there was a reporter out there as well, talking to Frownie Cop and occasionally shooting distrustful glances in my direction while taking his notes. This reporter was actually the very same Andy Carlson who'd so rudely vultured Sydney at Josh's funeral. And he was on the hunt for another juicy "human interest" angle for this piece (of trash).

It was rather unpleasant to catch snippets of their discussion about me. But that unpleasantness was nothing compared to what came next.

It was time to face my aunt and uncle.

Sal and Jem came bounding through the outer doorway, nearly bursting with anger and grief, respectively. Pam saw them the instant I did, and she jumped up immediately, shoving herself in front of her dad as he stalked toward my cell.

"Dad, listen to me. You've got all this so wrong right now," she was saying.

But he was undeterred. "Oh, I'm just sure I do. You're as bad as your mother." Which statement made poor Aunt teeter dangerously near to her default sadness mode of flowing tears.

I was ready and waiting as he approached. I stood at the door of my cell, forcing myself with nerves of melting steel to stare Uncle Sal in the eye. And in the mere seconds of him staring wordlessly, infuriatedly back at me, all I could think was how I had so been hoping it would not come to this. If only Sydney could have been here by now, before my only living family members had the awkward task of disowning me for a crime I didn't commit.

An officer stood beside them, informing them, "We'll be moving him to juvenile hall soon."

What! That was news to me, and it sounded terribly official and final. I tried to catch the rest of the officer's words about just how "soon," but it was difficult over the din in the lobby.

I couldn't help but gulp and glance once again toward the door. But no one else was entering, no Sydney blowing in to speak up and save me. Instead:

"That's fine, great," Uncle Sal said gruffly. "We're done with him." And to me, "You're on your own from here."

And Sal turned, storming off. Leaving Aunt Jem, poor thrice-broken Aunt Jem, to stare at me in near despair. I looked back at her, on the verge of breaking myself.

It seemed cruel, all of a sudden, my silence. To her, anyway. And I almost had to say something, to give in. I opened my mouth to.

And I couldn't. Because even a word to her would be proclaiming it to everyone, and I would be spilling Sydney's story to the world in an instant.

My aunt turned away, crumpling into more tears, to follow my uncle out of the building.

When suddenly, the door opened one last time. I almost didn't dare to look. Because if I did, and it wasn't her, I thought I might just lose it. But after a second that seemed to last ten minutes, I dared to.

Sydney.

She stood just inside the door, staring at all the people.

At first, no one seemed to notice her. Except for Uncle Sal as he was awkwardly trying to scoot past her out the door. All the other participants in this particular scene, the police officers and clerical workers and the occasional crime witness, none of them cared.

For my part, I held on to the bars of my cell, leaning forward eagerly, hopefully.

And she looked at me. We locked eyes. And I knew, with the same certainty she had known driving here, that everything would be okay.

I was conscious that Pam had just spotted her as well and was about to scream at the girl to spit it out. I murmured a, "Shh," and put out a staying hand toward my cousin, as Sydney took a deep breath.

And behind her, Sydney's parents were running in from the parking lot, Maryanne still holding the charred papers, which she'd glanced through as Robert had sped after Sydney through the Seattle streets. The paper's contents had really only served to confuse them further on what the truth really was—were these stories all made up? Partially so? Did Josh actually rape her? And if so, where in the bloody hell did I fit in to all this?

But, unsure as they now were of my guilt, they weren't yet convinced I was innocent, either. Sydney figured as much, that her parents weren't here to have a polite and casual listen to what she wanted to say to the world. So it was now or never.

She screwed her eyes shut and yelled at the top of her lungs, "Calvin Wilde is completely innocent. Josh Simpson raped me and fathered my child the night of April second, before Calvin and I ever met."

And she opened her eyes again, to the sight of numerous staring, awkwarded-out gazes.

Behind her, her parents had paused. Still doubting, but also one heck of a lot less certain that they had been correct this whole time, to see her this determined.

Uncle Sal and Aunt Jem had stopped in their tracks, utterly horrified. While Pam was all but dying with relief. I motioned my cousin over toward them, and Pam surprised me by going right to her bowled over mother with a hug.

I was aware that the reporter was scribbling out his notes and writing new ones as quickly as he could, while Frownie Cop meanwhile was just sighing angrily and leaving.

But this was all in my peripherals. Because I couldn't take my eyes off Sydney.

She finally had the courage to raise her eyes to mine again across the way. And I felt myself breaking into the biggest smile of my life.

Empowered, she stepped farther inside. "It's true. Let him out. We're dropping charges."

An officer looked to her parents. Who looked at each other. Then at their daughter. Poor Robert and Maryanne really didn't know what to think at this point. Robert said, "Sydney? How sure are you?"

She turned and looked her father in the eye. "Absolutely sure. You have to believe me. I know what I'm doing, and I know what happened. He's completely innocent."

Maryanne knew her daughter, even if Robert's cold intellectual nature did have a hard time reading Sydney's sincerity and emotion. Maryanne put a hand on her husband's shoulder. He looked at her, and she nodded.

So Robert looked back at the officer and nodded to him.

And finally, they let me out.

Sydney noticed the reporter. "And the press is here, perfect. Another juicy story about me. Maybe get your facts straight this time. But go ahead and write it all! It's a hideous story and everyone might as well know the truth about me and my freakish life. Because I can't change it."

By this point, free of my cell, I had advanced near her. But not too near. And I couldn't help cheesily telling her, "You just did."

Slowly, she smiled in response. Our eyes met. And we had a moment. One more of those lovely moments when all feels right with the world.

And, her parents moved in protectively. Moment ended.

But that was okay, because her father was actually hugging her. She turned to look at him. And suddenly she burst into tears against him, crying, "Daddy."

And he stroked her hair, murmuring, "Shh, it's okay," like any father might. He'd finally learned how. Maryanne moved to join the hug, and Sydney finally let her.

I stood there watching it all, so relieved I all but peed myself. When I realized there was still drama aplenty going on beside me, as Pam continued explaining to her parents. "There wasn't any reason to tell you and make it all worse!"

Pam was nearly crying herself, and my snotty mess of an aunt was saying, "I know, sweetie," as the two of them held one another.

And Sal, meanwhile, turned back to me. "Well don't just stand there, unless you want me to kick you out anyway."

I felt a sigh escape me as I turned to follow him, wondering what a healthy response to all this might actually look like.

But on my way out, I met eyes once more with Sydney. And from the middle of her long-overdue family hug, she mouthed to me, "Thank you."

I nodded back, a sincere smile on my face, feeling like the harrowing journey I had just undergone was absolutely nothing to accomplish such a beautiful end.

21

BUT THAT WASN'T THE END. Not by a long shot. It was merely the beginning of our story.

What followed was a mix of beauty and pain, joy and suffering as we dealt with the emotional toll that these events took on all of us.

I had what seemed so long ago determined myself in love with Sydney, when in fact I barely knew her at all. And of course she had spent the entirety of the time she knew of my existence extremely creeped out by me. Then add in my relation to Josh, Sydney's parent's attempt at my arrest, and a whole school full of gossips. Talk about a mess. There were moments not long after all this where I think we both must have thought it would be better for everyone involved if there was a way that none of us ever had to see each other again. But that's not the way life works. And despite the messiness of it all, I wouldn't erase it.

More importantly, though it took her some time and a *lot* of therapy, Sydney came to a place where she didn't want it erased either. The journey to that place was long and hard, but thankfully I was a part of it. The two of us grew, slowly at first, into friends. I longed for more but waited patiently to pursue that further as her trust grew. I fell more deeply for her by the day; the more I learned about her, the more I wanted her to be my wife. Obviously not yet, but I knew deep in my heart that it was meant to be. If we could survive the events we started with, I felt we could survive anything.

And, by the time she was eight and a half months pregnant, the two of us were finally well on our way. All was lovely. I wouldn't say it was perfect, for my beloved girlfriend was pregnant with my dead cousin's baby. But the big hurdles standing in the way of our being happy together were gradually falling away. Heck, even her parents had welcomed me into their house, which was definitely something.

In truth, I think they were rather relieved to see their daughter engaging in what was at least a bit more of a regular teenage social life, especially after her falling out with Winnie. As a bonus, she and Pam actually started to become friends as well. It turns out that Pam's snarkiness was at least as good a fit for Sydney's quick wit as Winnie's ditzy personality had been. Probably better, if we're being honest, especially considering that Sydney and Pam had both just undergone a very similar world of pain. Increasingly, the three of us would hang out together, and it was really as close to that lovely, familial quality time we each craved as any of the three of us had had any time in recent memory.

As for Sydney's relationship with her parents, I wish I could say that all was perfect there after the cathartic hug in the police station, but of course it wasn't. Things were much improved, to be sure, but they still had trying moments, their misunderstandings and their exasperations. Sydney did begin to realize that they were more or less doing their best toward her, and perhaps the maternal hormones in her blood were serving to soften her harsh feelings toward their failings. And on their part, the two of them both had to come to terms with the fact that their respective shortcomings as parents probably had contributed to things getting so muddled in Sydney's life at the get-go of everything.

Beyond all that, though, they did approve of me, for their daughter. A marvelous feeling, and one I'd been beginning to doubt I'd get to experience, for a while there.

Our plans for the future were slowly developing. I had been accepted to the University of Washington just around the corner, starting winter term a few months behind most of my peers, thanks to the disruption of only arriving in the country in April. In the meantime, I was taking a couple filler courses at a community college while working a part-time job. I was planning to major in engineering. All well and good, but the impressive one was Sydney. She was having a play produced professionally, was writing for several online publications, and was speedily breezing on her way to a writing degree at UW as well. While pregnant.

Her parents, after the initial shock of everything, had gradually grown to become thrilled at the upcoming birth. While the circumstances were obviously terrible, the two of them were very excited to become grandparents earlier than expected. In fact, they had always wanted several children but had suffered from poor fertility and been lucky to even end up with Sydney. Maryanne was beside herself in a flurry of planning for the upcoming new outlet for her hovering, and even Robert was emoting over the matter more than was his custom. And the two of them were more than willing to help Sydney with providing for their new grandbaby in any way needed.

As for Sydney herself, she was doing okay with it. She was scared, understandably. She never wanted to think of Josh again, and there was no telling with certainty that this child wouldn't be the spitting image of him in looks or behavior. But that feeling of certainty that all would be well had never really left her. After a little time off for mental recovery, she was now able to write again, and her playwriting success seemed a good indication that she was stronger than ever at it. But these days, she was sticking solely to fiction, rather than that dangerous mix of fiction and reality. And finally, she was able to feel that this child, as ridiculously out of her plan and ideas for the future as it was, was hers. Her baby. In a strange way, her recompense for all that she had suffered.

And I was ready to stand beside her, through life. If there was one thing I knew, it was that this child, not mine by blood but mine by love, would never be a lonely, fatherless child as I had been. He would never feel that someone had not wanted him.

We were ready. Except, she wasn't due for another two weeks.

Babies, apparently, don't really follow a schedule too well, because it seemed that it was ready to be out of there.

I got the call at four-thirty a.m. on a Thursday morning and was already on my way as Maryanne and Robert helped a violently contracting Sydney to the car. It was nippy out, and Sydney absently noticed her breath coming in puffs as she tried the breathing like the lady in the super retro '80s labor video we'd watched (and mocked) together. And she cracked a small smile at the remembrance of our laughter—a smile cut short by the vice-like pain in her lower abdomen. But it was okay. She knew this was going to hurt like hell, and she felt prepared, confident that all would be well soon.

I felt the same way as I sped to meet them at the hospital. Smug. That's what I was. We had it all figured out. Except …

Except, then I was in the room with her. And it was awful. Bloody, freaking, awful. She was writhing and sweating and doing her best to hold in agonized screams. Her father had had to leave, and Maryanne was pained as she stood beside her.

I never wavered from my duties of hand-holding, but I felt like it. Sydney was the one with the truly awful job, but it was harrowing to see her doing it.

Hideous. And beautiful. As it was always meant to be.

The OB was down at the end of the bed, saying, "You're doing great, Sydney. One more push."

And Sydney strained, wringing the bloody life out of my hand because it felt as if her pelvis was exploding and being torn to bits. She was shaking, and from the very depths she cried out, "Oh God! Oh God!" And it was anything but a curse.

And finally, at long, long last, we heard the cry.

Sydney collapsed back onto the bed, and Maryanne was teary, and I couldn't stop saying, "You did it, you're done, love. You did it."

And all Sydney could say was, "My baby. My baby," even as the OB was getting it a bit cleaned.

"A healthy baby boy," the woman announced.

I gasped. Sydney had wanted it a surprise. A little boy. He would be my son. Though not technically, he already was.

I got to cut the cord. And I nearly started bawling like a baby. I would care for this precious baby boy. And he would never know the pain of having an uncaring bastard for a father.

The doctor handed the baby to Sydney. Momentarily, Sydney was ginger with him, a little bit afraid. But then instinct took over, and she held the baby boy to her chest.

And then Sydney's tears came.

After all the pain, all the terrible things, here was one more. A terrible, beautiful thing that would probably continue to be a bit of both throughout our lives.

I knelt beside the hospital bed, this time a bed of life, not death. And I snuggled in for a closer look at our baby. I kissed Sydney's cheek tenderly, and I kissed the baby's little head. And the woman I loved snuggled her head back against my shoulder.

The three of us sat there, and in some terrible but beautiful way, we were a family.

Acknowledgements

Thank you to my loving and supportive husband Luke, who has encouraged me every step of the way in my writing career.

Thank you to my sister Alycia Youngquist, who has taken the time to read a few different versions of this story over the years and has given me valuable feedback each time.

Thanks to Jerry Windley-Daoust and the Gracewatch Media team for their refreshing honesty and transparency as a business (a breath of fresh air after dealing with the film industry!), and for their willingness to take a chance on my novel — just when I most needed a win after years of screenwriting rejection.

Thank you to Regina Doman, who worked to edit a very early version of this novel with me nearly a decade ago and helped me to make a compelling story out of the novel I first tried to write at age fourteen.

Thanks as well to Tony Sands for his valuable feedback on the screenplay version of this story, which helped me figure out what the story still needed to work well in any format.

And thank you to God for blessing me with the cross of a storyteller's heart.

About the Author

Adrienne Thorne is an avid lover of young adult stories and has been writing them since her preteen days. After graduating from Franciscan University with B.A.s in communication arts and theology, she delved into the world of professional screenwriting. But recently, she's taken a brief break from the soul-crushing rejection of Hollywood to return to her first love, YA novels. Adrienne lives in the Seattle area with her wonderful husband and growing number of small children.

More Gracewatch Media titles you might like...

In the Realm of Mist and Mercy

A STARMAKER BOOK

When young Waljan of the Wood is forced to move to a new home in the city, his first instinct is to resist everything about the change. However, it isn't long before his new circumstances put him on a collision course with the evil lurking in Mortinburg, as well as his own true identity . . . an identity that will only become clear if he can somehow discover what lies beyond a mysterious, unassailable wall just outside the city.

Be Yourself! A Journal for Catholic Girls

A MISSION:CHRISTIAN BOOK

"Be who God meant you to be, and you will set the world on fire!" Those words are at the heart of Be Yourself! A Journal for Catholic Girls, which is designed to help girls explore their identity and purpose in life in light of the wisdom of the Catholic Church.

Lectio Divina for Teens: Reading God's Messages to You

A MISSION:CHRISTIAN BOOK

Did you know God has written you a letter? It's "hidden" in the sacred Scriptures. The Scriptures are God's word for his people, the Church. But he also uses them to speak a special word to every person who seeks him there. *Lectio Divina for Teens* introduces you to the ancient prayer practice of lectio divina in a guided journal format.